SHE WHO REMAINS

RENE KARABASH

DESIGN & LAYOUT Sandorf Passage
COVER DESIGN Sarah Schulte
PUBLISHED BY Sandorf Passage
South Portland, Maine, United States
IMPRINT OF Sandorf
Severinska 30, Zagreb, Croatia
sandorfpassage.org
PRINTED IN THE UNITED STATES

Fourth printing

Sandorf Passage books are available to the
trade through Independent Publishers Group:
ipgbook.com | (800) 888-4741.

Library of Congress Control Number: 2025936874

ISBN: 978-9-53351-574-8

Also available as an ebook;
ISBN: 978-9-53351-575-5

This book was translated with financial support from the
Bulgarian National Culture Fund.

SHE WHO REMAINS

RENE KARABASH

Translated from Bulgarian
by IZIDORA ANGEL

SAN-
DORF
PAS-
SAGE

SOUTH PORTLAND | MAINE

Sworn virgin: A woman in the patriarchal societies of Northern Albania, Kosovo, Macedonia, Serbia, Montenegro, Croatia, and Bosnia and Herzegovina who has taken a vow of chastity under the Kanun of Lekë Dukagjini—a collection of archaic Albanian laws—so she may begin life as a man and paterfamilias. This is a constitutionally recognized gender transition, sanctified through a swearing ceremony, which bestows upon the woman the rights and freedoms of men, liberties she's heretofore been deprived of, and liberties all other women are still deprived of. Blood feuds are characteristic of the regions governed by the Kanun. Presently, because these societies have become largely unpeopled, only a few sworn virgins remain. It isn't a myth or a fairy tale; it is real human history.

Other names for a sworn virgin: *ostajnica*, *mushkara*, *vergjinesha*, *mushkobanya*, *harambasa*, *zavietovana devoika*, *sadik*, *burrnesha*.

still in my mother's womb
I hear things
like my father saying
iskam sin[1] */ I wish for a boy*

when I come out of the womb I learn
blue means boy
cause mama once told me
darling girl
your eyes are blue like the sky
and the sky was blue
blue must be a color
the color boy

1 In Bulgarian, the word *sin* (син) is a homonym. It means both "son" and "the color blue."

from the moment I'm born
I want mama to dress me
only in blue
and I weep
when she puts me in anything but
because still in my mother's womb
I hear things
like my father saying
iskam sin / I wish for a boy

today mama
put me in a blue dress
I crawled to my father
to show him me
and he said
hold on, let me listen to the news
which must mean
I'm very beautiful

I don't understand,
can you tell me what this means:
hold on, let me listen to the news
and then this:
breaking news
a girl hung herself
with her umbilical cord

PART ONE

Now Cain said to his brother Abel, "Let's go out to the field." While they were in the field, Cain attacked his brother Abel and killed him.

Then the Lord said to Cain, "Where is your brother Abel?"

"I don't know," he replied. "Am I my brother's keeper?"

The Lord said, "What have you done? Listen! Your brother's blood cries out to me from the ground. Now you are under a curse and driven from the ground, which opened its mouth to receive your brother's blood from your hand. When you work the ground, it will no longer yield its crops for you. You will be a restless wanderer on the earth."

Genesis 4: 8–12

The Heralds of Death

"The Kanun was mightier than it appeared. It reached everywhere, crawled on the ground, along the plotlines of the fields, it slithered along the roads, around the markets, made the rounds at the weddings, scaled the alpine pastures, then reached higher, reached the sky, whence it returned as rain, to fill the watercourses of the fields, the reason for a good third of the bloodshed." —ISMAIL KADARE, *Broken April*

my brother sends his best
says Nemanja's brother and shoots his gun just once
my father's warm body tumbles into the dead leaves,
his big eyes fixed on him, my father's big eyes locked into
Nemanja's brother's eyes, his strong hands grab my father
and turn him to the setting sun, he's exalted by the sight of his
fingers in blood, wipes them on Murash's shirt, the heralds
of death spread the news, *they shot Murash, Murash was killed,*

Murash was felled next to the wild pomegranate trees, next to the pomegranates, Murash, Murash, Murash, my mother wails and sinks into her skirt in the middle of the road, *Murash, my life*, the wind carries the howls of the heralds, the howls catch up to my mother on the dirt road leading up to our home and knock her down to the ground, she sinks into her skirt on the dirt road leading to our house, four broad-shouldered men stride up the dirt road to our home, carrying my father's body on four beech-tree branches, the road is uneven, the pallbearers' bodies are bent, they trip over their feet, my father's body rises and falls like a cough, they set the body down at my feet, it no longer moves, now I'm bound to ask everything the Kanun decrees, I have to ask the pallbearers what I must ask them, I open my mouth, only hot air escapes, hot air into the cold stares of the bearers' faces, the hot air that is no longer escaping my father's lips, come on, Matija, they mutter into their collars, avoiding my eyes, they don't wish to see the death of the father reflected in the eyes of his daughter, they'd rather see death in the eyes of the man than in the eyes of his daughter, they want to lie in their beds tonight unperturbed, yet I have to stand, self-possessed, I clear my throat and I ask what have you brought me

a wound or death

Bekija

I swear to the ruler of the Albanian Alps, Lekë Dukagjini,

that to my dying day, to my dying day I shall not touch a man, I shall not touch a man and I shall preserve my virginal innocence, renouncing for all times the woman in me

renouncing forever the woman in me

I will submit to this oath before God, I shall not succumb to the wicked desires of the flesh, and today, before the twelve-man council of elders, I shall take the masculine name Matija as my only given name and may the women cut off my hair and may my dresses turn to ash and may the clothes of a man become one with my back, my legs, my skin

my back, my legs, my skin

I swear, for as long as I am of sound body and mind, I shall keep my oath, fastened together with my hair and my honor, as God, and these fathers, are my witnesses

I, Matija, the son, will look after my family, I will provide for them all that is needed, all that the Kanun decrees as necessary, for sloth is the enemy of the soul, and I will henceforth, at appointed hours, occupy myself with manual labor, for only when I live off what my hands have borne can I be a monk of principle, and if I shall blessedly keep this oath, and suppress indecent acts and not break my word, then may I enjoy a life that is long and may I be surrounded by universal reverence, and if I violate and desecrate this oath, may the opposite befall me

in the name of the sky and the earth, this stone, this weight and for this bread

I am sworn

Matija

I exit the church and for the very first time I feel the ice-cold Albanian air with my head, I must resemble a shorn donkey, my braids lie on the church floor, to part with something you've had forever turns out to be easy as the wind, now they'll burn my dresses too, down to the last one, except for my future wedding dress, the one my grandmother gifted me before she died, together with a pair of patent leather shoes, she'd laid out the dress next to the clothes she'd picked out for her funeral, come here child, she said, I want to give you something, but grandmother, I said, there are two dresses here, which one is for me, she and I were the same height, she died after she slaughtered a sick baby goat and its blood poisoned hers, here, my child, she said, take this as dowry for the wedding, both dresses were beautiful, one was a red velvet, the other sky blue, I went for the blue one, the shoes were shiny and white, Bekija you took the wrong dress, put it back, this one I've picked out for when I depart this earth, no, grandmother, that's the one I like, I hate red, you take it, here, take it, I never wore that dress, it's still in the cupboard with the white patent leather shoes, I hid them before my oath so they wouldn't burn them, I almost wore them once, at my wedding, it was set to take place at the same church where my female self and I got separated

there's no turning back now

I exit the church and for the very first time I feel the ice-cold Albanian air, I must resemble a shorn donkey, so what, I tell myself, the most precious metal in Albania is freedom, around here a woman's worth is measured in oxen, don't look men in the eye, don't go to the pub, mind the children, wash the clothes, cook, the most women can hope for is to bring the milk to the dairy, Bekija's murder is the smartest thing I ever did, they gave me a shotgun and a watch, now I could smoke and drink and move with the men, go to the pub and visit the men's social clubs, they teach me to stand like them, legs apart, the kids in the neighborhood begin to call me *bate* Matija, I roam the narrow streets of the village every night practicing my new walk, getting used to it, getting used to overcoming my worth, getting used to wearing a watch, daddy's boy

your father wanted a son, but out came you

shush, mother, Matija appeared on the same day, I just waited for him to undress me, to dress me in his clothes, to put his watch on my wrist, there's no more Bekija, her hair floats in the river, do you know what, Mrs. Journalist, we, us people, need rules and boundaries, I think it's precisely what we need, I don't know what it's like where you're from, but here freedom is a dangerous thing

the whole village knows
Murash wanted a son, but it was a daughter he got

they all want sons in these lands, it's the blood tax, it's killing the men and there's no one left to look after men's things, I take the man's name, Matija, as my one and only given name

I exit the church and for the very first time I feel
I walk home, I must see whether the dress and the shoes are still there in the cupboard, the Accursed Mountains stand on all sides of me, the Albanian Alps, the Accursed spread out across thousands of kilometers, it doesn't matter which direction I head, there's the rooted army of evil rock, mobilized by the hands of the devil, the sky leans on the soldiers' shoulders, do you hear the cowbells—the evening church bells of the village, and then rain, not cascading but misting, it rains incessantly and it won't let up, it's raining now even as I speak, and fog, always the fog, densest here in the plateau, it's all a gray painting, neither melancholy nor blissful, how should I put it, like a face without an expression, you know what I mean, right, if only the rain were to cease, have you been walking a long while, it's like this here, you walk a lot, the roads are tangled and endless,

only the locals know the way, like the blind, they never get lost in the dark either

from the church I take the wolf trails home, on my left the river follows me the whole way like a strange silent satellite, suddenly it dawns on me what I've done when my strides become longer, bigger than my own and I trip over the rocks, the ubiquitous rocks, there's no turning back, I can't reattach my hair or swallow my words or blow up like a bullfrog and croak out the truth once and for all, out of nowhere through the fog I see the foundations of a house, I've seen it before, my father and I have walked by it, but for the first time I can't tell

is this house being built or demolished

The Bluest Boy

Matija, Bekija according to my passport, thirty-three years old, yes, one brother, Sále, father, Murash, murdered, mother dead shortly after, there's only Nura the cow and my father's pigeons, favorite color blue, afraid only of snow, the big snow, loneliness is another thing altogether, no, here love is forbidden, love is death, I don't go to the doctor, I plug up my wounds with tobacco, if anything happens I smoke, television doesn't exist, I don't need it, the radio is enough, Albanian songs and occasionally an American one, I can't sing, no, and I don't want to, this one here is of me, my father, my brother, Sále, and my mother, it was taken before, yes, that's enough for today, Nura is hungry and the pigeons need to be shut in for the night

The Twins

still inside my mother's womb
I hear things
like my father saying
iskam sin

my name means she who survives, she who remains alive, she who saves herself

something smells rotten here, what hospital, asks my father's mother, my mother carries twins, a boy and a girl, I am the girl, and the boy, my grandmother's words inside my mother's head, nothing good will come of this, the whole village is hissing, she's not carrying like it's a boy, it's all gotten out of hand, my mother bleeds in the bathroom, Murash, come here quick, she doesn't know if her two children are still alive or if they've returned whence they've come, my father's mother's incantations, this girl shouldn't be born, maybe it'll just be the boy, to carry on the bloodline, you don't want a girl, Murash, the whole village is whispering, *Murash's bride is having a girl, yazak*, what a waste, my father still certain that out my mother's stomach the worthy heir to the bloodline will appear because when you really want something to happen, it will, for

all desperately desired things materialize
one way or another

my father grabs my mother by the hand and off they go to the city hospital, just in case the twins are still alive, Mrs. Journalist, mothers here get pregnant in the hope of bearing boys so they don't bring shame to the family, they get pregnant in the hope that it will be the male blood of the kin sloshing inside the boy's broad trunk, that it'll be a man to whom they'll wish all the things they wish men here, *may you be blessed with a long life, let it be a shotgun that takes you down*

here every man must carry his honor on his forehead, two fingers wide, just like a bullet

a leaden hole in the head to elevate you beyond ordinary death, it's a matter of honor, it's shameful to succumb to illness here, not sure how it is around your parts, I expect the same, how could it not be, here vendettas are postponed only by war, natural disasters, epidemics, or migrations, when death loses its altitude blood feuds become the norm, *just don't let it be inside your house, Murash, that woman of yours, don't let her do this inside my house, look out for this one, son, she'll throw fire in your lap, I see her squinty little eyes, you know what that whole Karabash clan is like*, my mother—the black sheep of the family—is bleeding out in the bathroom, something smells rotten here, the blood in the bathroom, right, the hospital

the doctors do an ultrasound, he's not there, they're certain, what do you mean he's not here, the male one isn't here, he's gone, disappeared, how can he disappear, you've bled him out, my precious son, I can't go back with only her inside of me, please, doctor, do something, bring him back, I'm sorry madam, your husband is waiting outside, should I tell him, no, luckily, the female fetus is looking very good, better than good even, if she continues developing as she has thus far, you'll have a strong and healthy baby girl, which is why you must avoid heavy lifting and doing anything physically exhausting, you'll need to be on bed rest until the end of your pregnancy

I told you, Murash, this one here won't give you a boy, shut up you old witch, whatever comes out is my blood, it'll be mine, I'll raise it, my father's mother is throwing curses out in the yard, the village pretends not to hear, the village never hears anything but it sees everything

my father and my mother sway home through the screes of the Accursed Mountains and cry, why are you crying, aren't

I alive, doesn't my name mean she who survives, she who remains alive, why are you crying

my father didn't touch me for the first year of my life, avoided me in the house, didn't speak to me, I can't touch this worm, I'll crush it with my paws, look at how tiny it is

all desperately desired things materialize
one way or another, inescapably

daddy's boy, that's what my father called me, he knew his boy would be my clone, the same hair and teeth, the same height, fingers, eyes in blue, she's a natural, Murash, yesterday she nailed the cart-rails, she's got a knack for everything, strong and quick, she thrashes like a young colt, faster than the eye, the work's always done, no son would have been so dutiful and so adept at everything

my first memory of my father, he comes into the room, blacks out the window with his body and stands before me, takes out a wooden pistol from the inside pocket of his fur coat and hands it to me, here, Bekija, take this, I'm ecstatic, it's the first thing he's ever given me, the first words he's ever said to me, I start laughing, raise the pistol, point it at his head, squeeze the wooden trigger, and shout *pa-pa*, it's the first time I've ever seen my father laugh, now we're both laughing, both of us toothless, laughing, *pa-pa-pa, pa-pa* if only I could have told him then what I was yet to learn, if only I could have told him not to laugh, for the thing he wished for, it would come, just like the end of days

it shouldn't have happened that way

I'm asking you to have some patience, do you eat hominy, I'll tell you something, Mrs. Journalist, when you're done eating, do not wipe your plate clean with a crust of bread and do not put wood on the fire, that's my job, if you do either of these things I'll be forced to kick you out, kill you even, that's how the Kanun works

The Guest

arc you recording
now are you recording

I remember every word of the oath, Mrs. Journalist, and don't think it was something I had to learn by heart before I spoke it in the church, I've attended so many advents of transition, in other villages too, you absorb the oath whether you like it or not, something like those burial hymns, the same dirge at every funeral, only the musicians change out when one dies and another comes to take his place, if you were to listen to the same funeral chant every other day you'd learn it too, a lot of men die here because of those blood feuds, the blood tax, everything revolves around the Kanun, and according to the Kanun a guest is held in the highest regard, you, now, are my guest and you are of the utmost importance, the guest is revered here in Albania, the guest comes first and then the family, the house belongs to God and the guest, if someone were to knock on the Albanian's door, he is bound by duty to welcome him in, feed him, the wife washes the guest's feet, makes his bed and lays the fire in the stove, the following day the guest is seen off, and if it so happens that someone should be waiting outside to ambush the guest and kill him, what I mean is, were someone to kill your guest outside your front door, after you've seen him off but before the guest has turned his head, if your guest were to still be looking at you, you would be bound to avenge his murder, it is your duty to spill blood in the name of your guest, do not be afraid, no one here wants to kill you, you're not in a blood feud with anyone in the village, and besides, you're a woman, women don't enter into blood feuds, no one will seek revenge against you because you haven't killed anybody and you're a woman, right, and you're my guest, Mrs. Journalist, you stay here for as long as you like, that's how it is in the Kanun, you haven't killed anyone and neither have I, I haven't killed anyone

silence

did you hear me, Mrs. Journalist, there are two things the guest hasn't the right to do, wipe clean their plate with a crust of bread and put logs on the fire, if you were to do that, in that very moment, right as you see me standing before you, I could get up, open the window, and yell out to the village that I've been slighted by my guest, and then I could kill you, but don't think I would, why would I need to kill you, how many people have you seen in the village since you've been here, three, you'll see maybe three more, I am the last remaining sworn virgin in the village, maybe even in Albania, isn't that why you're here, whom am I supposed to show off my celibacy to, why have I been living alone this entire time, my most trusted friend, Nura, the cow, by my side, most of the elders died off, only five remain, to settle the vendettas, wait a minute with your questions, there'll be time for everything, from you I want just one thing, you see that box on top of the dresser, over there, open it and bring me what's inside

The First Letter

Hello, Bekija,

I very much hope this letter reaches you. I know the houses in our village don't exactly have numbers on them, and I'm aware of how impossible corresponding through letters and telegrams can be. I have been meaning to write to you for a long time. Every day since I ran away . . . You must understand why I had to do what I did. Why I ran. That I did it because of the enormous, irreparable mistake you made. You do understand it is completely within the bounds of one's survival instincts to want to save oneself, right? My leaving was the smartest thing a sane and sober-minded man could do, someone unafflicted with the delirium of the laws of the Kanun. I can't apologize for it, it is who I am.

I don't regret running away, just as you don't regret becoming a sworn virgin. Either way, a feeble and delicate person like me, a *gevşek*, does not deserve to walk upon the ancient, hallowed lands of the Kanun. These lands are all one big funeral feast anyway. Murder is pride and honor, isn't that right, *daddy's boy*, and for weaklings like me there's only one open door—that of the Kanun. It's why I chose to exit out of another door altogether. If I'm being honest, you were the only person who ever truly understood me. I still wonder about what it is that makes us so alike and yet so different from each other. I turn and twist it around in my brain like a math problem I knew the answer to long ago as a child but as time went on, I somehow forgot.

Why did you pick me to die? Why did you tie the black armband on me and sentence me to death? It mustn't have been easy for you to do—to choose one of us to die, Murash or me, eeny, meeny, miny, moe, just like we played when we were little. Who will the spinning dervish come for? Remember, you always won. Why did you tie that black armband on my arm? I believe I know why. I know more than I wish to know, but I still want to hear it directly from you. What happened that evening you went to the dairy for milk and came home late for dinner? The same night you told Murash you wanted to become a sworn virgin and back out of your wedding? Something happened that night. What was it?

I know you're angry with me. You're angry I ran away and Murash had to die. There are a lot of things I'm also angry about, but I hope with time, forgiveness can become ever more possible. I'm hoping my letters won't upset you so much that you won't want to write me back. I would love it if you came to visit me so we could look each other in the eye and tell each other the truth, the way we did when we were children. Truth or dare? Back then, we thought the weaker always chose truth because they were afraid of being bold. I realize now that picking truth was always the braver choice. Dare was for the liars, the cowards who masked themselves behind their bravery. For those who preferred to jump in the river, to run away, or to kill instead of telling the truth.

Please write me back. I really hope you kept up with your Albanian lessons after I left. You learned to read, right? I'm waiting for your letter. My address is on the front of the envelope. I'm quite worked up over everything, I'm sorry, I'm sending you love and hugs. Please tell mother I love her . . . Not a day goes by that I don't think about you both.

As you can see from my address, I live in Bulgaria now. Here I go by Mihail. I thought that if I changed my name I'd be able to somehow change the past. But this is another delusion people tell themselves and I fell into that trap. We remain enslaved by our real names and actions. To the very end.

Sále
July 8, 2017
Sofia, Bulgaria

Sále

my brother, Sále, was a post-term baby, born when I was a year old, *a son is born*, my mother said, there were little skins hanging from his fingers, like cotton, *cottonings* she called them, a blue boy he was, looked as if he'd hung himself with his umbilical cord, but out he came, nonetheless, I learned to count using my brother's ribs, that's how scraggy he was, hey Murash, how nice you finally got a son, a bag of bones, if the wind blew it would blow him away, what sort of son have you borne me, woman, a mannequin from Buchenwald, Bekija's got more muscle than him, daddy's boy, and this sonny boy here, so feeble yet growing up smart, only five and learning to read and write, doesn't get too excited about guns and things like that, reading his grandma's Neckermann catalog all day instead, learning about stitching so they can sew together, how repugnant, shoot, Sále, the rest of the time he's up on that landing, wriggling around with his grandma's shawl, dancing, he calls it, you hear me, kill the goddamned bird that's eating my maize, we're the laughingstock of the entire village, I forbid you to dance, my father caught a little sparrow in the dovecote, it had snuck in through a tiny hole he'd forgotten to plug up, he handed the gun to my brother, *shoot*, the sparrow was tied to some twine wrapped around a rock big as two fists and it was flinging itself up and down, the sparrow would go up and the rock would budge a little and then the sparrow would hit the ground before again trying to lift itself up, *shoot, you fool*, I could not look at my brother, he'd never killed before, I felt shame when I looked at the little bird too, so I nailed my gaze to the rock, which budged a bit every time the small creature attempted to spread its wings, *come on, Sále, show us, did your mother birth a son or a floozy*, my brother stood, shaking, the gun pointed at the ground, I stopped looking at him and stared at the rock, you know how it is, you sink into the ground from shame or pity

the gun went off, I heard a yell, then some unintelligible swearing from my father, after the gun went off I could no longer hear anything, a thin rivulet of blood ran down my father's calf, my brother had shot him through the leg, my father then grabbed the gun and killed the small bird himself, my brother couldn't move, stood frozen like a rock, his pant leg wet, his face unmoving, not even crying, fuck your mother Karabashka, get the fuck out of here, *gevşek*, go weave your lace, you motherfucker, he's gonna shoot *me*, the dirty shit

I'm staring at the rock on the ground, the rock no longer budges, the rock is red

Green Water Red Rock

Sále frees the rock from the twine
the rock looks like a little ladybug
he raises it above his head
he slams it down on the green walnut, he slams it
down on
Murash's head sticks out over the fence
Murash is chopping the neighbor's wood
Sále crushes walnuts, one after the other
he's shoving walnuts in his mouth without shelling them
first
he fills his mouth and leaves no room for another
walnut
the walnuts have not yet ripened and they dye his hands
black
their green skins shatter under the rock
green water sprays Sále's legs
darkening his skin where the specks land

tiny freckles on his milk-white ankles
Sále shoves walnuts in his mouth
Sále shoves death in his mouth
the sparrow to the cats, my mother says
and splashes a bucket of water where the floor needs it

Sále throws up
Murash's head no longer sticks out above the neighbor's fence

Murash

my father sucks on the boiled cockerel's neck

it's thin and bony, filled with juices, the air whistles through its cavities, clear juice trickles down my father's chin, travels down to where his shirt splits in two, the juice oozes down, splits his chest symmetrically in two then disappears into his lap, leaving a tiny wet spot, my father's leg is bandaged up, there's a red stain on the white rag, my brother is chewing on a scrap of bread, the crust is dry, it can't be gnawed through, it gets lodged in his throat, my brother is not hungry, my brother glutted himself on too many walnuts, the crust is hard, it obstructs his throat, he extends his black fingers to the glass of water, takes a gulp, the water washes the inside of his mouth, carries the crust down, dissolves it into a mound of soggy crumbs, my brother swallows, the gulp reverberates in the room, the curtain rod rings out, my father is no longer sucking on the neck of the bird, my father stares at my brother, he still sees the thing that happened today, the air is no longer whistling through the cavities, out in the distance you can hear the clops of the mules, my mother is not breathing, my mother cannot remember what breathing is, Murash raises his hand over Sále

Murash,
my mother sighs from underneath the floor

Murash bangs the table with his fist, the plates jump, this rotten Karabash seed, Sále gets up and goes to the dark of the garden, Sále goes back to his rock

the red stain on the gauze widens

Dhana

after I was born it came to me
blue means good, blue means boy
my mother once told me, my sweet
girl
your eyes are blue, blue like the sky
and the sky was blue, so blue must be good

Bekija, go fetch the sandpaper, it's in the trunk above the washbasin, next to the razor, this dovecote won't build itself, every day he shaved over this washbasin, patted his face dry with the towel, then slowly, carefully wiped the razor on both sides as if he were sharpening it, then pushed it into a crack in the wooden frame of the window, there's not much sun in Albania, there's more fog than sun, you see for yourself, Mrs. Journalist, but on that day, unlike most days, the sun was out, I went into my father's room, the sandpaper was exactly where he said it would be, I took it and looked into the small round mirror over the washbasin, the sun shone for the first time that year, I saw my father's razor stabbed into the window frame, a slim shadow rose from it and fell on my face like a mustache, dark and gluey, curving downward, I glimpsed myself in the mirror, could almost feel the coolness of the razor on my upper lip, my hand rose up of its own accord and my pink little fingers touched it, it's hard to describe what I felt in that moment, some kind of force, happiness maybe, I wanted my daddy to see me

it was like trying on new clothes for the first time, clothes that simply fit, weren't too big or too small, they just fit, I froze, the blue curtains billowed behind me, the pale mustached boy in the mirror stared back at me, he resembled Skanderbeg, the hero, my mother once showed me a photograph from before I was born, of her and my father in front of the monument of the great Albanian hero Skanderbeg in Tirana

somebody knocked on the window and I jumped, certain it would be my father, instead it was the great-granddaughter of baba Tsane from one street over, the girl lived in Bulgaria and came to the village for the summers, we were the same age but she was much taller and more beautiful, but no one ever played with her because she never said anything, Dhana with the translucent skin stood at the window, smiling at me, her teeth white, I still see them, fresh milk and shame, broad as shoulders, shame engulfed me and moved me one step to the right of the washbasin, the mustache stuck to the blue curtain behind me, I could still feel the shame, behind my back now, like some sort of presence, like a relative I was embarrassed by, I wanted to hide from her, here she was, staring at me with her white teeth, I had no idea what to do, ask her what the hell are you staring at, bitch, or smile back, I swallowed dryness, Dhana, quick, get out of here and go home, Bekija, where are you, get over here, the sun will be down soon, I looked to the door, then returned my gaze to the window but Dhana was gone, only her silhouette still lingered in my retinas, like an icon in the frame of the window, I squeezed the sandpaper in my hand and left the room, still seeing her silhouette wherever I looked, I shut my eyes, then opened them wide so I could see her again, but there was less of Dhana on each successive try, until she became a tiny dot I last saw burned into my father's forehead

Scars

today my mother
put me in a blue dress
and I crawled to my father
to show him me
and he said, let me listen to the news
which must mean
I'm very beautiful

where were you, Bekija, you're covered in flour again, I was playing with Dhana at the water mill, look at the time, you haven't even shut in the pigeons, and now the hawk snatched another one, the whole village won't shut up about how you can't stop dragging yourself around with Tsane's great-granddaughter

there's no fixing you since she showed up in the village

you'll do as I say, there are rules in this family and you'll obey them, don't hit her, Murash, she's your daughter, there are no other girls around, whom else is she supposed to play with, all she does is work for you all day, you shut your mouth, who gave you permission to speak when I'm talking to her, woman, you be quiet, what were you doing at the water mill, we were reading, how the hell were you reading when you can't read, are you gonna lie to your father, Murash, don't

my father's hand hangs over me like a bird of prey, my mother's skirt becomes suspended in the air, billowed by the wind of my father's hand, the clock stops, only screams and the pulsating vein in my father's forehead, I look him right in the eyes, look at me, it's me, daddy's boy, you can't strike your only son, you have no other son, it's me, Bekija, your daughter, my son, my father's hand clenches into a fist and shatters into tiny shards on the floor, the clock pulls the reins and returns me back to where I'd rather be

Dhana and I lie next to each other on the big millstone, we budge gently in the womb of the water mill, where did you get this scar, um, I was picking rose hips with my mother and the bushes scratched my face, what's your scar from, um, I was playing airplanes with my father, the game where I jump and he catches me, only he dropped me and I split my eyebrow

did you apologize to her
I apologized to her

did you apologize to him
I apologized to him

later we play a game, are you a rose hip, I am a plane, are you a plane, I'm a rose hip
our scars glow in the dark

we see each other for the first time

The Crucifixion

the following day the neighbors gathered outside our gate, chattering over each other, I heard laughter too, bravo, Murash, you made short work of that filthy animal, how many of my pigeons did that bird eat, we'd given up, I put on my vest and went out to see what the clamor was all about, I got chills, there on the gate was the hawk, it hung off a handmade wooden cross, crucified by two nails pounded straight into its wings

the wind gently fluttered the bird's feathers but the wings did not budge

Nemanja

the coffee's right over there, help yourself to some sugar, I prefer it black myself, there's *popara* under the towel, on a morning just like this one my father

what are you staring at that rock for, you're going to be a bride, aren't you happy, Nemanja comes from a good family, it's about time too, the Kanun might even say you're too old, you're a woman of marrying age, but I don't even know him, you will get to know each other in time, but Jelko told me all about him, he said he was very ugly, there's no such thing as ugly, Nemanja will give twenty oxen for you and a sack of grain for each ox, they've got a television just like us, his brother's wife says only good things, she's not gonna say anything bad, she's one of them, go get your things, we're getting you married the day after tomorrow . . . really, the day after tomorrow, that soon

really, that soon

even if there was a funeral taking place at Nemanja's house this wedding would still happen and even if there was a body at their house, they would carry it out so you, the bride, could walk in, and you—dead or alive—you're going, the second you give your word, that's how it's always been, that's how it was when the Turks were here during the occupations, that's how it was during the First and the Second Republic, it's how it is today and how it'll be tomorrow, the Kanun doesn't recognize the laws of time, my girl, don't let me hear a peep about it, marriage is business, love is for the feeble, marriage cannot be broken after it's been entered into, so use your head

you said the day after tomorrow
I said the day after tomorrow

you know I'm required to put a bullet in your trousseau, it's what the Kanun says, and Nemanja will kill you if you're not pure, you are pure aren't you

I am pure

don't cry, Bekija, you won't find anyone better, says my mother and splashes a bucket of water where the floor needs it

The Wing

when I was a little girl I helped my father with men's work, I still remember the day he built the dovecote, the neighbor had gotten his hands on a pair of pigeons and offered them to my father as a thank-you for slaughtering his calf, you want bean stew or these two pigeons, give me the pigeons, my father muttered under his mustache, you chose right, neighbor, these two here are Serbian Highflyers, built for endurance, Serbia's national treasure, brought into the country during the Turkish yoke, they can fly four hours at a time, my father brought them in the house in a small cardboard box, don't you dare pluck these birds for soup, woman, Murash here has lost his mind, his faithful friends discuss him at the pub, the herbalist gave him two pigeons and here he is, building them a house in his grandfather's shepherd's hut where he slept to guard his sheep, that's what I heard too, he cleaned out the hut, put in nests, whitewashed the walls, put a fresh coat of paint around the windows and the doors, put in a lock just in case, my father enters the pub and the latches on his faithful friends' faces go *click*, they all grit their teeth and kiss Murash's hand, Murash, Murash, tell us all about your pigeons, they've not flown yet, I tore up their wings just yesterday, pulled out every other feather so they can't get up too high or gather too much wind, otherwise they'd fly out, I've shut them in the dovecote now so they'll settle into their nests

the most precious metal in Albania is freedom

I haven't left the village in I don't know how long and I don't need to, everything I need is right here, the only thing that weighs on me is that I've nobody to talk to, there's only Nura, the cow, or a neighbor, young people my age are long gone, sometimes I talk to the pigeons but Nura seems to understand me better, here, let me show you something

you see that pair of birds, they're Turkish Tumblers, they've got a beautiful aerial game, turning and twisting and flying, my father watched them for hours, playing, one day a Turk was passing by the house in a cart piled with birdcages filled with pigeons, dad bought the Tumblers, he went crazy for the feathered ones, a pair of Macedonian Rozanne, those white ones on the birch tree over there, a male and a female Archangel, the shiniest ones, do you see over there, the one with the rings on its back, he's alone now, I'll tell you something, Mrs. Journalist, the Turk also sold my father a pair of Baska pigeons, the ones with the really short beaks, those guys can barely feed themselves with those short nibs, they need their own feeder, these ragged ones here were the very first pigeons we got, they're in their dotage, hardly fly anymore, they just walk around on the ground and graze, the rest of the pigeons are in the big dovecote behind the house, it's the one my father built before he died, the pigeons started laying eggs and hatching so fast the birds ran out of room and began to fight over territory in the dovecote, but my father could never bring himself to throw out their eggs, as he was leaving the Turk gifted my father a tiny dove, a thank-you for buying that many birds, *it's all alone anyway*, it was a brown cuckoo-dove, and you know something, Mrs. Journalist, it's quite interesting, it's got a very different song, like a cat meowing, like that story about the owl of Minerva I was once told and it's why I called it Minerva, people on our street always thought they heard an owl but they never saw it, then they found out it was coming from our house and when the real owl came, they paid no attention to it and it's why death sometimes passed by the village, though not always, my father gave me the bird, here have this teensy one, Bekija, a little dove just for you, because you're always helping me and doing what I ask of you

daddy's boy

I told my brother he could pet the small bird as much as he liked, you're not like your brother, you're strong, tough, daddy's boy, we worked on the dovecote all day, at dusk we washed our hands at the outdoor basin one after the other and sat down at the table, my mother had boiled a hen "red salt-style," it's what we called my father's favorite meal, you season the boiled bird with a brick-red rub of salt, sweet paprika, savory, fenugreek, and thyme, eat, Murash, this hen's for you, you worked all day, you're exhausted, you need your strength

I'm not hungry

Sále, mom, and I sucked on the bird's soft sweet bones, Sále less so, my father sat with us at the table and only drank rakia, he'd breathed in paint fumes and felt nauseous, he said, he glanced at the hen in the pot, I read revulsion in his eyes, and when he felt my gaze he turned his head and looked out the window, as though he were running from having his mind read

what are you staring at

did he think someone was going to go inside his head and find out what he was thinking, what was he hiding from us, my brother hid his hands under the table, somewhere in the distance a mule brayed, my father sipped his rakia, licked his lips and again fixed his eyes on the pot but now there was nothing but a pile of bones from some feathered animal, what kind, you couldn't tell, my mother washed the dishes, behind her back a pile of bones, behind her back a pile of death, all the chicken's bones, sucked to a glisten

except for a wing, outlined in my brother's pocket
its grease stain slowly spreading

In the Dark of the Hallway

you're too capricious
you won't amount to anything

it's alright, my mother tells Sále, my father used to tell me the same thing,
she tears a slice of bread in two, smiles, and hands him the bigger half

The Milk-White Bride

there are things you can't foresee,
like the fog
a familiar song slips its tongue under the
door of the dairy
it's him, Kuka the Hook, the village idiot

dogs and carrion in ripe blackberries
heat in the calf's gut
a bronze horse chews olives
a hook and a cross in the cut

is that you, Kuka, I thought it was Hasim, only he comes to the dairy this late, is that you, it's him, my heels go numb, the dusk swells in my throat, the shadow in the doorway keeps singing its song, Kuka slowly closes the door, the dusk is now inside, fully inside me, my body its last resting place, it has gripped my throat, a silver glow enters through the dairy's tiny window but it's blocked by the man coming in, by his song

the eye of the water snake is a hook, my love
the eye of the water snake is an ear

I haven't seen you in forever, Kuka, is it milk you've come for, I've just poured ours out, ten and a half liters, is your cow still alive, didn't she die a few months back, my body is a moth nailed to the wall by the pins of his eyes, eyes black as olives, eyes of tar, pupilless, bodiless eyes, I cannot move

the water snake is hungry, feed it
come on, milk-white bride, douse it

the shadow moves toward me quietly singing its song, its back blocks the light and it cannot reach me, the milk whitens the copper vat, it still ripples because I've been drinking from it with my hands, there's still milk dripping down my elbows, only two more steps and the shadow will overtake me, I start for the door but the shadow blocks me, I go west and it's already there, I go east, there it is again, I tighten my braid

Kuka, I'm being married off the day after tomorrow, are you coming to the betrothal, words fall out of my mouth, didn't your cow die a few months back, I can't stop talking, it's what you do with crazy people, to rid their heads of crackpot thoughts, but what I'm really doing is holding up, holding up what's bound to happen, what's already happened, it's just that in this dairy, time lags

snake resin hook
snake resin hook

I can feel his breath on me, he's drunk milk before he's come here, the village whispers that at dusk he enters the goat barn and drinks milk straight from the goats' teats, there's other things they say about him but I don't want to know, Kuka is now right next to me, he stands over me like a stone pillar, I'm a moth, nailed to a brick wall by the pins of his eyes, his eyes don't glow in the dark because coals glow only when you've set them on fire, his eyes are black as though they've been gouged out, or the person behind them has been

Kuka, don't, let go of me

go play with the other boys on the hill, I saw them on my way here, they're still

there, playing tipcat, I'll go home and won't tell anyone that you were here

I shouldn't have said that, Kuka's strong arms encircle my waist and we plunge toward the copper milk buckets, we fall and the buckets clang like church bells, the milk buckets are our wedding buckets, my dress swims in pulp of milk and mud, the buckets ring to the beat of the rider, *ding ding ding ding* then faster *ding ding ding ding* get off me, motherfucker

Kuka's hand clenches my mouth, Kuka's hand is now an inextricable part of my face, I take this hand and this stranger's body as my own, *ding ding ding ding*, I am no longer in this scene, I am witnessing everything from outside of my body, my hair swims in the warm milk, my eyes stare into a small hole in the wall, which moves in beat with the galloping horse, I've never seen it before but there's light coming through, the hole in the wall, yes, I see it for the first time and from today on this hole exists because I see it, the hole hurts, it hurts

are you pure
I am pure

don't cry, Bekija, I hear my mother say, let whatever hurts you remain here, and the milk of life floods my black dress and the church bells fall silent, the snake is fed, I close my eyes

the eye of the water snake is a hook, my love
the eye of the water snake is an ear

after the breathing

Kuka stands up, tightens his pants with twine, his cheeks burn he smiles at me and looks at me, sees me for the first time, hi, Bekija, have you just gotten here, I touch where the wet is, I see blood on my fingers

are you pure, Bekija
I am pure
daddy's boy

how many liters did the cow give today, Kuka asks and starts kicking a little stone, playing with it, chasing it, kicking it like a ball, he's laughing and kicking, a child

a little boy who's worth more than twenty oxen, which is how much I'm worth, because he is a man, a real man now, whom would they believe, him or me, what do you think, there's no point in telling anyone, I stand up and lean over the milk, I splash my face with it, splash where the red is too, pink runs down my thighs, I tighten my braid, smooth my hair back

I know what I'm going to do
the little boy sees me and stops kicking at the stone

you're beautiful, let me walk you to your house, it's dark out already
no, Kuka, I'll walk alone

I can find my way home in the dark too

In the Mouth of the River

a voice whispers

wash yourself, drink water from your elbows, pour three handfuls of water in your bosom, wet your apron, and wrap it around your face

I see the shoes and the dress from my grandmother, the best man and the best woman lead the wedding procession, we walk down the dirt road, the fog mixes with the dust, two mountain men go past us, they carry sacks on their backs, no, they're carrying two corpses, a man's and a woman's, they don't greet us, they stare at the tips of their shoes, I, bathed in blue light, in my patent leather shoes, with grandmother on one side and Nemanja, ugly, hunched and rawboned on the other, everyone who surrounds us carries rifles and pistols with muzzles that reach beyond the Accursed Mountains, the beat of the drum measures our steps, at the very end of the procession, my father and my brother lead the horses on foot, my mother next to them, weeping, behind them, mysterious women in black wail and pull at their hair and howl like jackals, am I getting married or getting buried, I enter the room of my beloved Nemanja, where are you, grandmother, can I lie down next to you for a bit, I lie down next to my beloved, he is handsome, in the darkness of the room, his face disappears and emerges again, is that you, Nemanja, I love you, Bekija, but you don't even know me, how can you possibly love me, the Kanun says I can, take off your dress, I take off my dress, everybody's hushed in silent expectation outside the house, their bodies frozen like stone, take off your shoes, I take them off, someone shouts *she's not pure*, the white sheet flaps out of the window, the bride's not pure, she isn't clean, she's not pure, she'll perish young, she isn't pure, my brother's crying, Bekija, my dear sister, my father strikes him across the mouth with the back of his hand, she's an idiot, she should have sat on her ass, Nemanja takes out the bullet from the trousseau, my father has placed it there before seeing me off, it's all according to the Kanun, if the bride isn't pure, she must be shot by the groom with the bullet given by her father as part of the trousseau, that's what the Kanun says, that's what the Kanun says, the women in black are pulling out their hair, their wails now vehement, they lacerate their faces with their nails, they want to take off their masks, to turn their faces, the hoarseness in their throats, their wet headcloths, I can't hear the goats' bells, I can't hear them, *you've got a hand of gold, Nemanja, shoot straight, shoot, my son*, Nemanja aims and shoots me in the chest, I feel nothing, I'm still standing, a red mark on my dress

am I dying or being born

it'll all be over now, Nemanja walks out of the house, everyone's quietly clapping, the village idiot comes into the room, is that you, Kuka, it's me, he lifts me from the bed and carries me out in his arms like a bride, now I can finally hear the goats' bells and they soothe me, Kuka cradles me in his arms and carries me toward the mouth of the river, the bells toll but these are not wedding bells, this is the funeral toll

wash yourself, drink water from your elbows, pour three handfuls of water in your bosom, wet your apron, and wrap it around your face

I wake up

I get out of bed, kneel on the floor, and pull out the box with the trousseau from under the bed, the bullet is there, on top of my blue dress, I am going to be married off, I take the bullet, walk out into the hallway, and put it in the pocket of my father's fur coat, I wake him up, I will become a sworn virgin, are you sure, I am, are you pure, I am pure

wake your mother and your brother, the wedding's off

The Black Armband

from the moment I'm born
I want mama to dress me
only in blue
and I weep
when she puts me in anything but
because still in my mother's womb
I hear things
like my father saying
iskam sin

Bekija, daughter, you've destroyed us, a sworn virgin, how could you, it's my wish, mother, then consider the groom's honor stained, you've gotten us into a blood feud, you've destroyed us, child, you've destroyed us, what do you mean sworn virgin, haven't we given you everything, what kind of devil has gotten into you, shush, you witch, it's her wish, so be it, the Kanun says she can turn away before the wedding and take the vow, she won't be the first or the last in this village, we will protect the family's honor, blood will be shed, so it shall be, the Kanun above all else, Bekija, choose, my father hands me the black armband

who says you can't touch death

you can, on the arm of someone condemned to die, the black band on the arm of every other man in the village, of everyone in a blood feud, of everyone who has to die, of everyone who has to kill, Nemanja must kill a man in our family to reclaim his honor, Bekija, choose, who will it be, me or your brother

my brother cries tearlessly, my father breathes heavily, the Kanun has finally seized him, swelled his chest with its highest decree, the law of honor, my father lifts his left arm, my mother cries, I look at my father's arm, if only he could levitate with his entire body for the honor of not succumbing to some disease or perishing in his sleep, now he will go marked by the two fingers of honor across his forehead, one movement of my arm and the painting falls to pieces, Bekija, choose, the air thickens, the ceiling slants downward

it wasn't meant to be this way

the water snake is hungry, feed it

milk-white bride, douse it

the thick beams close in over the heads of the two men, I take Sále's arm and tie the black armband around it, my mother sobs the way mothers sob when they've been told their sons have been killed in battle, her long petticoat sails over the room and wraps around the door like black smoke, the ceiling returns upright, the air thins, the breathing returns

Sále doesn't move, he's no longer trembling, he's not crying

Sále's already dead, that's why there's no breath left in him

keep your manhood, Sále, or stain it, let it be according to your will, my father says, kisses my brother on each cheek and exits the room

there's the son you always wanted, Murash, there, my mother wails in the cellar, her cry blackens the entire house, it passes through the beams, crosses the attic, blasts through the bricks on the roof and shatters one into the cement, the cat jumps into the shrub, my mother's howl shoots above the village houses and searches for an open window

The Hollows

out of all of us, the pigeons, me, my mother, and my brother, my father loved the Kanun most of all

it's why he always made sure everything went according to its rules, when he came to tell us that my brother had run away, he'd already tied the black armband around his upper arm, I can still see his eyes, proud but broken, in two days my mother had to survive my brother, my father, and Bekija but it's not like anyone ever asked her how she felt about anything

shade is shade, you notice it only when you need its shelter or when it stands in your way

I'm getting out of here

it's what my brother must have said to himself, I may have even heard him say it when I tied the black armband on him,

I can't recall, maybe he said it so only I could hear, countless other times he said it without ever opening his mouth, I heard him say it even before he said *babi* for the first time

even after my brother left, my mother kept setting out four forks instead of three

habit is the most treacherous thing in this world

Sále's pockets are always greasy, my mother does the washing at the basin in silence

when a mother stays silent, she knows, when a mother knows, she washes

silence sat in my brother's chair, in truth it had always been there, it sat in my brother's lap every time he ate, sometimes squeezing his throat and leaving him unable to swallow a single bite

fuck your mother Karabashka, go weave your lace

and don't you dare step foot on that cement slab for your stupid dancing, you creep, the whole village is talking, what is this queer son you gave me, a mannequin from Buchenwald, sometimes the load was so heavy it kept him pinned to his seat, always the last to eat his dinner or he got up without eating, Sále's pockets are always greasy

Sále's gone, he's run away

said the black armband on my father's arm, and he, leaden with the pride of knowing he's been entered into a blood feud, that he won't die of old age or illness, begins to sink weightily into the floor, the honor is mine, I'm going to build a new dovecote, bigger than the first, the biggest dovecote in Albania, beneath my father's feet the boards grind their teeth, the worms inside are bursting, looking for a crack to squeeze through, what do you mean gone, my darling boy, Sále, my mother clenches her mouth with her hand and squeezes it

outside the window, a brown rabbit hops from the bush, I pray my father doesn't see it, give me the shotgun, woman

the three of us sit at the table
me, my father, and my mother
there's bread, a roast rabbit, wine
and four forks

habit is the most treacherous thing in this world

Sále's chair sits empty, there's a shotgun propped on it, I glare into the floor, into two shoe-shaped hollows, a fly has landed inside one

it flies away

The Besa

the heralds had already delivered the news to Nemanja's family that there'd be no wedding, and his family then sent the heralds out to tell the whole village that Nemanja's brother would avenge the insult to his brother's name, he who raised his arm first did the avenging and it was Nemanja's brother who had first raised his, such was the law of the Kanun, this was the most perilous time because my father hadn't yet been granted the *besa*, the pledge of honor, the temporary stay, and Nemanja's family could shoot at any one of us, lock the doors, don't you dare leave the house today, I've fed the animals already, they'll survive without food for a day, at sunrise I'll send Preng to request a short besa, the avenger cannot kill during it, but as soon as the besa's over, there'll be an ambush, the short besa lasts twenty-four hours, Preng requested a short besa and he got it but the next day the village granted my father the long besa, a whole month, the long besa is granted after the funeral of the killed by the avenging family, but we hadn't killed anyone from Nemanja's family and there was no funeral and it's why my father had the right to a long besa, blood feuds are treacherous, families slaughter each other, exterminating all kin, the heralds spread the news about the besa to the whole village

the village had to know

it should always know what happens in the dovecote, its eye is all-seeing

they granted Murash the long besa, the long besa for the old mayor of the village, they granted him the long besa for his daughter, Bekija, she called off her wedding to Nemanja, she's taking the oath, becoming a sworn virgin, Murash's besa starts now, he'll be gone in a month, he's a dead man walking to death's door, the only thing my father said when Preng brought him the news of the long besa was, I want to build a new dovecote, bigger than the last, I want to build the biggest dovecote in Albania, it's what everyone does during the besa, they either fix things around the house, or, if they've got no wife, they settle down or they work on the land or they drink from dusk till dawn, swearing and swatting the flies at the tables

my father began building the dovecote and when I say that's all he did, it was all he did, from light until dark he hammered boards and forged and sawed and laid roof tiles and painted, he increasingly didn't come home for dinner, my father's life was now no longer broken into the before and after of his mayorship but into the before and after of the besa, and for him life converged into just a single matter—the dovecote

when you kill someone, you bring a blood tax of five hundred leka to the Elbasan Castle, you walk three days until you get there and you wait a week if you have to until they take your blood tax from you, it's where the *kapedan* is, the highest title in the Kanun, the prince, we are all his subordinates, the Kanun is impenetrable to laws, Mrs. Journalist, governments fall and others come in their place but the laws of the Kanun are made of bronze, it's no coincidence they're from the Bronze Age, I'm proud to live in these lands, I don't feel like talking about the solitude, freedom is more important, brothers and fathers don't matter when it comes to the Kanun, its laws stand above all else, above even those rock masses over there, a man's honor has weight, and so does preserving the family's honor

I'll build the biggest dovecote in the village, in the last days of the besa Murash worked later and later because time was dwindling and there was still much work to be done, the Loony who lives inside the goat house says that Murash sleeps in the dovecote and his wife wails like a jackal every night, the Loony sees him come out every morning as he walks to the goat house in the half-light, but Murash doesn't see him, I don't see anything, nothing, just the dovecote, my father enters the pub and the latches on the faces of his beloved friends go *click*

The Lament

in the last days of the besa my mother sleeps alone, I hear her delirious sleep-talking, calling out to each one of our pigeons by name

Archangel, where are you, rescue us pious ones

then I hear my father's name and after it I hear nothing

The Stag

I lift the shotgun and aim for the head

the body goes down, I hear it tumble into the wet leaves, its big eyes are locked into mine, it wasn't supposed to happen this way

well done, Bekija, that beautiful stag, my father comes toward me, looks at the still-breathing animal on the ground, looks back up at me, and slaps me across the face, his hand burns my cold cheek, he takes my gun and goes back in the car, doesn't speak to me all week, you don't kill deer and stags, how many times have I told you, these are noble animals, killing them is a crime, what's the difference between a rabbit and a deer, why is it okay to kill rabbits but not deer and stags, that's nature, nature is bound by rules you don't question, pour the last jug out and don't let me hear another word about it, I pour out the jug of burnt oil into the wide forest ditch, that's what my father and I did, a merchant who passed by our house sold us plastic jugs of burnt oil on the cheap and we poured them into the shallow forest ditches where the wild boars bathed so we could follow their tracks, either to the maize by the levees or to the hill facing Barganesh, some went into Uncle Stiche's lucerne, Murash, get over here now and bring your gun, they got in again, those motherfuckers, I'm on my way, we lie in ambush all night behind the bush or in the glen, there's no visibility at dusk, all you can see is the fog and the massives, the Accursed, and the cross on the wooden church, cocked by the wind, you sit, you don't move, and at dusk out of the fog a large dark shadow emerges, raises his shotgun and shoots my father in the head, my brother sends his best, the warm body falls, hollow, into the leaves, his big eyes locked into him, my father's big eyes locked into Nemanja's brother's eyes, well done, Bekija, you hit a good stag

at dusk a big dark shadow emerges from the fog, he's lain in ambush all night so he could kill him, he's rubbed his hands together to keep them from freezing, he's chewed on fatback and garlic, he's drunk rakia, he's waited for my father's big eyes to lock into the eyes of his killer, waited for my father to say something before he meets his maker, that's what the Kanun decreed, before you kill the person you've got to kill, you've got to tell him something, anything, good to see you, Murash, my brother sends his best or

daddy, I want to become a sworn virgin

The Second Letter

Hello, Bekija,

I still haven't heard from you. I really hope you are doing okay. I've been to the post office to check whether my letter got to you and they told me it should have been delivered by now. You must be feeling apprehensive about writing me back. Maybe that's the reason you have yet to respond. That's alright. You don't have to write me back if you don't want to. I will write to you. I've been silent for so long but I am increasingly finding it impossible to remain so. All the things I know are making it hard to breathe. Like giant lumps in my throat, making me feel complicit in everything that happened. Complicit in the murders you committed. Your own included.

Yesterday, the restaurant near my house served rabbit stew for lunch. I was certain it could not surpass our mother's stew. Eating the dish is what reminded me of the incident I can't erase from my mind, and which keeps coming back to me now and again. Do you remember when Murash discovered the wild bunny by Nura? Nobody could figure out how it was able to get into the cowshed but that didn't seem to matter very much. I knew Murash was capable of anything and suspected he might have caught the rabbit in the forest with the full intent to play a game on us, you know, the way he loved to invent games for us as a way to pit us against each other. Or rather, games that you, without fail, would always win. That was natural, you were far better at shooting than me. "Put the bunny inside a sock and put it near the stove so it can warm up." Remember? I'm not condemning Murash or doubting his intentions to save the animal, but you know as well as I do that he was equally capable of doing good as he was of doing evil things. I expected anything and everything from him. Just not from you. Now I can appreciate the fact that your actions have always been unpredictable. But back then I was little and trusted you blindly. Do you remember what happened with the bunny? I'm still wondering why you told Murash I was the one who killed it. I still remember it like it was yesterday—our mother called me to the kitchen to help her strain the milk and when I came back out, Murash yelled out my name, and you know what happened after, I had to sleep face down for two nights because it hurt too much to lie on my back. Last night, I tossed and turned the same way and I couldn't find peace, not because I'd been belted but because I was troubled by a single thought. All night, I couldn't get this out of my head: Why would you tell Murash that I was the one who killed the bunny? I finally drifted off with the dawn but I still had no answer to my question. It occurred to me that it wasn't enough for you to be "daddy's boy," you wanted to be something more, a daddy's boy who must save the rabbit from her brother's feeble hands. You were always our father's favorite. Murash had only one son: you. Nevertheless, things aren't quite so simple, sister. I will endeavor to make you understand that everything you did to become "daddy's boy" was for naught and that the Kanun is nothing but a fable shrouding you in a delusion of security. It will never truly free you.

I've been thinking a lot about forgiveness lately. I think our souls find peace when we are able to show forgiveness to one another. But before all that, there must be truth. I will ask you again: What happened at the dairy that evening when you returned home so late?

I await your response with eager anticipation.

Sále
September 19, 2017
Sofia, Bulgaria

The Lie Is a Worm

lies

are you going to believe the letter or me, it was one thing I wanted, it was another thing entirely that came to pass

it wasn't supposed to be like that, I wanted to help the animal, the way it was looking at me, a lie, I've got a stomachache now, will you give me that little brown bottle on the windowsill next to you, he killed it, the lie is a worm

kids, put the rabbit in a sock and keep it by the coal-burning stove to warm it up, it's freezing, my father enters the room, holding something in his giant palm, quick, I've got more work to do in the yard, Sále reaches out his hand toward our father, I reach out my hand for my father, both of us in one voice, give it to me, our father gives it to me, I feel the slight soft life in my hand, *put it inside a sock*, and I walk to the stove in small steps, my brother runs along next to me, let me touch it, he pets it, smiles at it, talks to it as one would to a human, asks it if it's got friends, pets it some more, quick, go get a sock I tell my brother and my brother brings back a big, gray wool sock from who knows where, red fabric sewn up for the heel, we put the rabbit in and . . . Sále, come help me strain the milk, mom, do I have to right now, Sále, don't make me have to repeat myself, he starts going out of the room and as he does, he looks back before disappearing across the threshold, I'm holding the sock with both hands, the stove is getting hot, too hot, it's burning my hands, wake up, little bunny, it's too hot, it's burning me, mom, it's too hot, wake up, little bunny, the stove, the rabbit in my hands, wake up, little bunny, the bunny is no longer freezing, the bunny is steaming

it was my brother, the lie is a worm

the sock falls to the floor, I kneel down, pick it up, stand back up, the rabbit is not moving, Sále comes back in, my brother, the stove, my father, right, the rabbit's dead, I kneel and put it back down on the ground, I stand back up, in comes my father, my brother, the rabbit, the stove, who killed it

Sále killed it, the lie is a worm

I kneel down, I take the dead rabbit, I hand it to my father, Sále killed it, Sále killed it, he suffocated it, then he kicked it into the stove, he was so rough with it, he said rabbits aren't free when they're among people and they have to be killed and eaten

Murash begins to weep from joy, grabs Sále by the face, kisses him hard on the mouth and lifts him up over his shoulders, my mother pins a sprig of wild geranium behind my brother's ear, Murash stands up, my mother is crying and caressing my brother's legs, my father takes off barefoot down the black dirt road of the village carrying Sále on his shoulders, my Sále killed the rabbit, my young Sále is a real man, daddy's boy, killed it with his own bare hands, kicked it right here with this foot, kiss his feet, the whole village walks behind them, the village kisses Sále's feet, the village is elated, the whole village is jubilant, every villager is throwing white handkerchiefs at the father and the son, wherever they pass through, the road whitens behind them, everyone's hugging and crying, I'll give you the shotgun, I'll give you the bullets, long live your son, Murash, may it be a shotgun that takes him down, the lie is a worm, one thing was meant to happen but it was another thing altogether that came to pass

you, you piece of shit, my father grabs his belt, I'll show you how you kill a small defenseless animal, no dinner for you tonight, go to your room, something's moving in the darkness of the garden, the next day my brother didn't utter a single word to me about it, as though nothing had happened, at one point I even thought I must have dreamed the whole thing because everything was as it always had been, my father and I took off to go hunting, Sále packed our backpacks, two pieces of bread, fatback, and green onion in my father's bag, some green onion and water in mine, we stood in ambush for a long time, nothing came, we sat silent the entire time, at some point my father said

it was going to die anyway
wild rabbits' littles can't survive alongside domesticated
rabbits, why, I don't know, he said, that's nature

so why did you bring it home, if you knew it was going to die
we'd better get going home, the rain is coming

The Third Letter

Hello, Bekija,

I hope that the reason you aren't responding isn't because something bad has happened to you. The post office told me you should have received my second letter as well as my first. I'm beginning to wonder, since I'm not receiving anything in response, if there's any point in continuing to write to you . . . So many questions are searching for a way to get out of my head. Whether I will ever see you again, whether you're even still alive . . . my darling sister . . . I'm doing my best to continue to hold on to the belief that you are fine, that one day you will come visit me and I'll be able to show you this other world, a world that's different from that of the Kanun.

When I arrived in Sofia, I had nothing but two sweaters, a single pair of pants, and a pair of shoes. You remember how I loved dancing on that slab of cement in our house and the kids called me a fag and threw rocks at me. I won't get into how I managed to cross the borders. I was beaten and robbed at the Serbian one. They took the only money I had. When I arrived in Sofia, I asked where the main street was located and that's where I headed. I put down the red cloth from mom on the cement tiles of the sidewalk. I began to dance, that piece of cloth was my sole possession, but at least I was free. And I danced. Nobody threw rocks at me. People stopped and left money. I don't know how long I must have danced but at some point I lost feeling in my legs and then in my entire body. As I danced I felt as though I drifted off to sleep. I woke up when someone splashed cold water on my face. An elegant man with salt-and-pepper hair held my head in his hands and wet my face with water. He turned out to be a professor of modern dance at one of Sofia's universities, and he told me he hadn't seen anyone dance like that in a very long time. We communicated in the little English I knew from TV. He told me he wanted me to join his dance troupe and to help him with his work at the university. He told me I had a certain "duende" about me. I didn't understand until later what he was trying to tell me. At first, I thought I was still dreaming, but then I understood. This man was an angel sent from heaven. He helped me with legalizing my documents so I could stay in the country, helped me find a place to live, signed me up for Bulgarian and English lessons and everything else I needed. In a few months, I was able to find my footing. I couldn't believe this was all happening to me. What had I done to deserve it? I was taught that I deserved nothing good and that I must always take the blame for everything. My memories from the past remained only in my dreams. At first I dreamed of Murash's belt. Sometimes I dreamed of standing guard with the shotgun meant for the hawk. Other times I crumbled the kernels of corn from the cob, the same kernels of corn Murash forced me to kneel on for hours on end. Slowly, the nightmares began to appear less and less. Then they came only as shadows and feelings, without images. One night I dreamed of you and Dhana. I will never forget that dream. You were both little and naked and you swam in a sea of milk. You were both laughing. Then Murash appeared and drank up the sea of milk with a sugarcane straw. Dhana turned into a fish and began to writhe on the dry land and you turned into a white she-wolf and ran off into the woods. The fish then grew wings and flew away into the woods too.

I remember the two of you. When it was you two, everything else disappeared, as though the world were made for the two of you and the two of you alone. One night, I hid at the water mill. I listened to her reading to you. She had the most beautiful voice I had ever heard. It is so sad that she left . . . There is something I need to tell you but you're not giving me any indication that you can hear me. I can't understand whether I feel the need to tell you all this so that a weight is lifted or so that I can open your eyes. Whatever the real reason, I want us to get to the truth. To find forgiveness for both you and me. Be honest with me. Please,

Bekija. Tell me what really happened that night at the dairy. Come to me and tell me, I won't judge you, let's start over. Like kids would. The way we would have back then . . .

Sále
October 12, 2017
Sofia, Bulgaria

stop recording
that's enough for today

БЕКИА

Matija
it doesn't say Bekija, it says Matija
my name is Matija, don't you see what it says
it says Ma-tija

Birthmarks

the words disappeared with Dhana and my brother, as did all the books from which she read to me during the summer vacations, when they left me, I stopped my Albanian lessons, I can't write, I can't read, I've read the most beautiful books in the world through Dhana's eyes, she read to me every night at the water mill, Dhana wanted to be a writer, it's why she was always reading and writing, and my chronic stomachaches, the ones I've had ever since I was little, the only time they went away was when Dhana read to me, that's when the pain disappeared, nothing else helped

the village is whispering, the village is saying that Bekija and Dhana meet up at the water mill under the pretense they're going there to read books, but who knows what they're actually up to, Murash, did your daughter never learn to read so she needs to go and get books read to her, didn't she get taught how to read at school

Dhana was my mirror, my medicine, my salvation, God had given us both tiny birthmarks right where our clavicles met, above the heart, so we could recognize each other more easily, and just as easily lose ourselves in one another

or lose each other, irrevocably

Babo Tsane, is Dhana not coming to visit, go on, girl, she isn't here, stop coming already, don't you understand

suddenly Dhana stopped coming to our village for her summer breaks, I never saw her again, I'm not sure what happened, what could have

suddenly

love, who here speaks of love, love around these parts is death

were you to choose love you'd be choosing death or death would choose you, but you're always the last to find out, before the pomegranates ripen and crack

The Wild Pomegranate Trees

my brother sends his best

they shot Murash, Murash got killed, they felled Murash down by the wild pomegranates, at the pomegranates, Murash, Murash, Murash, my mother screams and sinks into her skirt in the middle of the road, *my life, Murash*, the wind carries the yells of the heralds, the yells reach my mother on the dirt road leading to our house and knock her to the ground, they're carrying my father's body on four birch-tree branches, the road is uneven, the bent-over pallbearers trip over their own feet, my father's body rises and falls like a cough, they place it down at my feet, unmoving

come on, Matija, they mutter into their collars, avoiding my eyes, they don't wish to see the death of the father reflected in the eyes of his daughter, they'd rather see death in the eyes of the man than in the eyes of his daughter, they want to lie in their beds tonight unperturbed, yet I have to stand, self-possessed, I clear my throat and I ask

what have you brought me, a wound or death

my mother enters through the large gate and throws herself on my father, kisses the white face, the still-warm hands, she's been to pick wild pomegranates, a wound or death, she wanted to make him wild pomegranate jam before he went, the whole village is talking about how Murash had tried to follow her, where is your mother, at the wild pomegranates, it wasn't supposed to go down like this, he wanted to tell her something before he went, some kind of secret, only the two of them knew what it was, he had wanted to see her, to be next to her when the shotgun took him down, the whole village is talking about how male pigeons lose their minds when they lose their partner

a wound or death

death

say the pallbearers, my mother throws herself on my father and the pomegranates in her bag roll down the wet cement

you can't make jam from wild pomegranates anyway, mutters one of the pallbearers

they never really ripen properly

Black Headscarves

the soul of the slain cannot find peace until blood is shed in redemption

a good shotgun was shot
says the rebec player and hangs my father's shirt on the fence

when these stains yellow, the dead will claim his revenge, at Nemanja's house and at our house there are people coming and going, the yard blackens with headscarves, someone's loudly chiseling a cross into our front door, the pounding comes back like an echo from Nemanja's house, someone there is also carving a cross into the brown door

the black headscarves wind along the road like a swarm of ants, the black headscarves are scratching at their faces, they want to tear off the faces from their headscarves, they follow behind the cart where Murash lies, his arms crossed, elbows propped up by two rocks to keep them from sliding down, he looks like he's praying, the black headscarves are wailing, they can't take off their faces, their rubber shoes sink into the mud, the black headscarves do what they have to do, it's why they're here, to mourn the dead man, the cart is pulled by the gravedigger and the stonemason

the rain is coming

says the gravedigger to the stonemason, I've not taken in the sheep, says the stonemason to the gravedigger, I turn around and look at them, then I look at my mother, the shadow next to me carries the cross, behind the black headscarves, like a tail, the drummer shuffles in his wool house shoes, the drum's skin is blackened where his drumstick has struck, he's the only one left, the others have passed, says the gravedigger to the stonemason, there are no people left, and soon, judging by how this one here's dragging his *terlici*, we won't even have a drummer, a fly lands on my father's forehead, the gravedigger throws the last shovel of dirt and leans the shovel on the cross, the stonemason hands him a cigarette, spits to the side and says

us it passed by, but it got the sheep
one of them is thrashing like it's got the staggers, I'm gonna have to slaughter it one of these days

Nemanja and his brother sit at my dinner table, they've come for the funeral feast, that's how it is according to the Kanun, the killer sits and eats with the killed one's family, I put the bread on the table and sit down, Nemanja's brother stands across from me, between us steams a rabbit stew, they've sunk their faces into their bowls, whoever might be peering through the window won't see the heads of the two brothers, the bodies are feeding at the table with no heads, the rabbit stew steams before them, their bodies smoke, the gunpowder has exploded, their shoulders move like the shoulders of a rawboned jackal stalking a rabbit, a fly lands on Nemanja's hand, he swats it away, the same fly from my father's forehead lands on Nemanja's brother's hand, he stops chewing, his mouth full, his cheeks puffed up, filled as if with stones, his nose whistles when he breathes, he deftly traps the fly with his left hand, squeezes it into his fist and throws it on the floor, the fly falls into the same hollow in the floorboard that resembles someone's shoe

outside the window, a brown rabbit hops from the bush, I pray for my father to see it and to say to my mother

give me the shotgun, woman
but the two chairs gape like rotting teeth in the cavity of the room
I know there won't be new ones growing in their place

Nemanja and his brother stand up and use their right sleeves to wipe their mouths in concert, they leave our home and the blood feud continues, now one of them has to die, from the bullet in my father's pocket

marriage or funeral—a wound

but sworn virgins cannot kill
the blood feud is dead

The Razor

the peeling mirror over the washbasin

the holes on it mark my face, I lift my head, stare at the spot where the apple of my throat rises, I press the razor right into that spot, from the time I was born I heard certain things, from the time I was born, I've been waiting for this, this touch that will erase the past for good, I squeeze the razor, you're getting what you deserve, one thing leads to another, everything that happened is the truth, isn't that right, goodbye, Bekija, the razor descends down Bekija's right side and glides the foam up Matija's neck

Bekija, go fetch the sandpaper, I hear my father say,
this dovecote won't build itself

it's probably from the mirror, I feel the coolness of the razor on my throat, my hand moves it slowly, if he could only see me now, on the second month after I took the oath my period stopped coming and never returned, soft dark hair grew on my chest and my neck, I began shaving and the hairs turned hard and sharp, I feel them each time I run my hand over them, just as my dad did

daddy's boy

my father's razor and Dhana, staring at me with her white teeth, her silhouette is still there, engraved in my retinas, the icon framed by the window, I towel my neck dry, I lift my head and check whether I've missed something, of course, here it is, I always miss something, this time too

I've missed something again, I've missed the opportunity not to shed blood

The Light

read me the last letter and go home
go on, open the envelope, here's the bread knife

my heart begins to gallop like a doe being chased by its own shadow, there's a second envelope inside the letter from Sále and it isn't from him, don't tell me

the ceiling starts to crumble, small pieces of plaster fall on my head, one piece splashes into my coffee, leaving a black stain on the tablecloth, read, it says Dhana, the envelope says Dhana, read, no, first the letter from Sále

the glass in the windows shatters into salt

now the letter from Dhana

the wall facing the road collapses entirely, the room turns bright, very bright, the light is impossible to bear because it is sudden, you can't run from it even if you close your eyes, it's still there, so intense that for a moment you feel as though you were seeing light for the first time, that up until now you've lived in darkness

you can't look at me, Mrs. Journalist, you wouldn't be able to see me anyway, because I am no longer here, I have disappeared into the light, I am drifting within it

you're ashamed, I make you uncomfortable, the moment has come, you must leave now, and let me be alone with the light

nobody deserves this, nobody deserves to be read these letters or to hear them, mere pieces of paper that shatter windows, pieces of paper that bring down walls, after these two letters there'll be no one left in this house anymore, this house does not deserve its inhabitants, this entire time, all these years, the house has stood silent, holding its severed tongues locked inside the letter box, all while I lived here, holding them unbeknownst to me, I knew nothing for so many years, nothing

this is what happens when you think your life is worth more than the lives of others, when you realize you were the worm inside the apple all along and you've been rotting ever since, and all the apples around you have been rotting too

I wonder whether there's even a God, whom have you been praying to, was there anyone there to hear the little rock falling in the well, it's all my fault, if only on that night I hadn't

this was it, it was all over

if the other three walls of the house were to fall, I wouldn't even hear them

I can no longer hear anything, I can only see this piercing light, the light which floods my body in waves

am I dying or being born

I Now Know

I am the red rock in Sále's hands
the stream of blood on my father's calf
I am my father's shoe imprint sunken into the floor
my bleeding mother
the bloodied shirt in the yard
the lamb hanging from the walnut tree
lightly swinging in the wind
Dhana's red cheeks
the cheeks whose dimples I sank into and never left
once

and for all

I Will Depart

sixteen years ago I killed Bekija
today I will kill Matija

the cow bellows, my things burn in the middle of the room, the wall has collapsed, hasn't it, so I lit a fire inside, inside is now outside, the fire spits photos and letters to the ceiling, words burnt to ashes spiral around me, the heads of my mother and father soar above me, black moths, they turn to dust the moment they touch down, the fire's hot fingers caress me, I sit draped in my father's fur coat, and in its inside pocket the bullet

why did it all go down like this

my father's fur coat, the bullet in its inside pocket, a passport, a dress, patent leather shoes, shoes like prosthetics, I topple with every step, a scarecrow, the heads of my mother and father soar above me, black moths, they turn to dust the moment they touch down, Nura's bellowing disarms me, I clench my teeth and tell my neighbor *two big bowls of feed before sunrise, a bale of hay at night, and a bucket of water, that's it, do what you want with the milk, take it to the dairy if you want, make cheese if you like, you know how to care for a cow*, the neighbor nods, she knows how to care for a cow, Nura looks at me with her big, wet eyes, steam escapes from her nostrils, when are you coming back, the cow's bellowing disarms me, I clench my teeth and say nothing, I say nothing, what you're witnessing is a murder, I think it but do not say it, I wave her off and she walks away

there's one thing left to do, I have to unlock the pigeonholes, I go to every door and turn each latch backward, unlocking it, turning it in the direction of the past, this small, insignificant thing that I do twice a day is now a triumph, on this day now it is a ritual because I am perhaps doing it for the last time, I set the birds free, though I know they won't fly away, pigeons always return whence their first feathers were clipped

home is where they clip your wings

the road winds upward, I refuse to turn and look back, whatever happens I owe myself this at least, not to turn back, to keep going up the rocky path, to part with something you've had forever turns out to be a breeze and still your body turns to the command of nostalgia, my home—my fortress, my prison, from this height the house resembles a pile of rocks, the dovecote throws its shadow on the house, there's my father, hammer hammering away, do you hear all that nonsense coming out of Murash's mouth, I'll build the biggest dovecote in Albania, the house sits in the shady mouth of the dovecote, you can see it only from up here, from the distance, where I stand right now, before the jagged cliff, before I continue on upward and before everything is to remain behind my back

I am departing

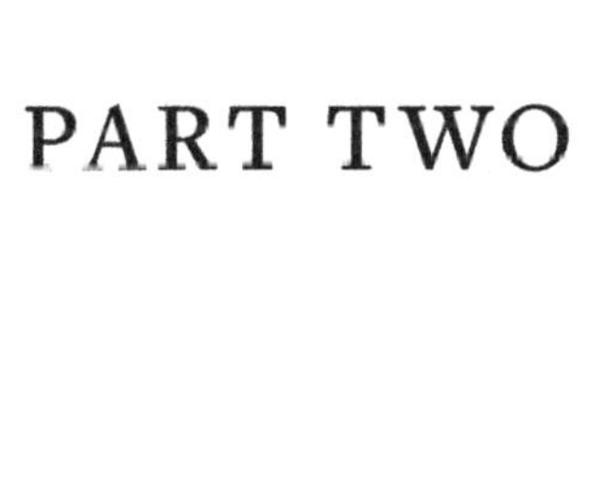

PART TWO

That which has been, is, and that which will be, has already been —and God will call the past to account.

Ecclesiastes 3:15

Muted Milk

the path twists like a water snake
ever farther from the past and ever closer to it
the bus rocks my body as though there were no body in it
I hear a familiar song on the radio

dogs and carrion in ripe blackberries
heat in the calf's gut

the lie is a worm that lives inside of me and a familiar song slips its tongue under the door, is that her, it must be her, someone told her I'm here and she's come

a bronze horse chews olives
a hook and a cross in the cut

is that you, Dhana, I thought it was Nemanja, only he comes to the dairy this late, is that you, it's her, my heels go numb, the dusk descends, the shadow at the door continues to sing its song, her white teeth gleam in the darkness, it's her, you shouldn't have come so late, you'll get in trouble with your grandmother, Dhana slowly closes the door behind her back, I swallow spit and milk, a silver crescent of light comes through the small window of the dairy and illuminates she who enters

the eye of the water snake is a hook, my love
the eye of the water snake is an ear

when did you come back to the village, Dhana, I'm glad to see you, did you come for milk, did your grandmother send you, I just poured ours out, ten and a half liters, how much milk did you get from your cow, Dhana doesn't answer, she steps toward me and with each step she sings, my body is a moth, nailed to the wall by the pins of her eyes, eyes green like seaweed, eyes like little frogs, eyes without a body, pupilless eyes, bodiless eyes

you are the only one

the song is closer and closer to my ear, the milk whitens the copper, it still ripples because I drank handfuls of it before the door opened, there's still milk streaking my elbows, two more steps and the green will cover my entire body, I don't move to the door and even if I did she would stand in my way and not let me leave, I know her, her arms will encircle me and I will be forced to die in them

ever closer to me

the bars on the window paint a cage on her face

I tighten the braid in my hair, stop, I have to tell you something, Dhana, they're marrying me off the day after tomorrow, my father wants me to marry Nemanja, I don't want to, but that's how it works in these parts, will you come to the betrothal, I want you there, please, Dhana's eyes fill with the sea and the seaweed pales to white but she doesn't stop moving toward me, she smiles with wet cheeks and sings, I know

come to me my darling, fill my hands with your face

I start to cry too and I begin to speak, will you be there, forgive me, I can't stop the words from falling out of my mouth, that's what you have to do when you've told someone you've just killed them, you have to keep on talking so she forgets what it was you've just told her

I speak and I delay, I delay that which is bound to happen, the thing that Dhana has come so close to me for, it has all happened already, time in the dairy flows backward, even the milk reverses the direction in which it flows

Bekija . . .

I feel her breath, she's drunk milk before she's come, the whole village is saying that Bekija and Dhana meet up at the water mill, to read books, they say, but who knows what they're really doing in there, Murash, did your daughter never learn how to read that she has to go and get books read to her, did her school not teach her to read already, get your things, we're marrying you off the day after tomorrow

is it really the day after tomorrow, my love

it's really the day after tomorrow, please come

she's so close to me now, right next to my heart, I am a moth nailed to the mud-brick wall by the pins of her crystalline gaze

the day after tomorrow, you say

for the first time in my life I taste life, life is biting my lower lip, and I say *ah*, then her body pins me to the wall, and I say *yes*

have I even lived, Dhana's long arms encircle my waist and together we fly toward the copper buckets of milk, we fall to the ground and the buckets clang like church bells, the copper milk buckets are our wedding buckets, my dress swims in milk and mud pulp, the buckets clatter to the rhythm of the female rider, *ding ding ding ding*

I love you

Dhana's hand muzzles my mouth, Dhana's hand is now an inextricable part of my face, I take this hand and this body as my own, eyes overflow, desire lacerates our faces with its teeth, digs its claws into our backs, it's been sitting like a beast waiting to emerge, lying hidden in some dark corner, secretly wetting the millstone while she read a book as I listened, I don't know, if we let go, will we ever untangle

don't let go of me

Dhana's doughy thighs grip my body like pliers, her fingers disappear into the pain at the bedrock of my body, the wave rises inside of me, lifts me then topples me, a scream and then a gasp

am I being born or am I being murdered in her arms

Dhana kisses my eyes, kisses my mouth, then she stops and buries her face in my hair, *I'm leaving*, I already know what this is, this is the end of the world, I still remember her salty kisses and the small hole in the wall I'd never seen before, when Dhana cried out loud, *I'll find you*, the last of the daylight drained away from it, and the moment we left the dairy, eternal night would come for the both of us

am I dying or being born

Dhana gets up and fixes her hair, her cheeks burn

she smiles at me, my beautiful angel smiles at me, the road twists, ever farther from the past and ever closer to it, hello, Bekija, hello, Dhana, I touch where the wet is, on my fingers—blood

I will love you forever
I will love you forever

I get up and lean over the milk, I splash my face with it, I splash where it hurts

I tighten my braid, I smooth my hair back

I knew what I had to do
I had to bury Bekija
because she was killed that night
the road turns like a water snake
ever farther from the past and ever closer to it
the bus rocks my body, as though some body wakens in it
the radio plays a familiar song
something is sprouting inside my stomach but I have no idea what it is
whether it's a flower or a weed

The Fourth Letter

My dear sister,

I understand now that there is no chance I'll ever get a response from you and it's why I've decided to tell you everything I was keeping for when we saw each other in person. I had the strong desire to hear the truth directly from you and for us to ask each other for forgiveness, but it seems I'm the one who has to ask for it first.

I know what happened the evening you went to the dairy and were late coming back for dinner. As much as I didn't want to, I witnessed everything. You know how much I loved to follow you around, I even trailed you in secret sometimes. That evening, I followed you to the dairy and stayed outside. There was a small hole I often liked to peek through. I closed one eye over the hole and knelt down. Everything felt like a game, just like every other time, until Dhana came into the dairy. I saw everything. I still remember the song she sang, I remember the words she spoke. The most beautiful words I had ever heard. You remember them, don't you? "The eye of the water snake is a hook, my love, the eye of the water snake is an ear." I'm not sorry that I was there and saw what happened, otherwise I never would have gathered the courage to run away after you tied the black band on my arm. Love gave me the strength to do that. You knew Nemanja would shoot you because you were no longer pure, so you decided to take the oath and become a sworn virgin and choose death for me instead. This made me think of myself. You probably already know why I did it, the same reason you did. To save myself from certain death. At the price of someone else's life. Murash's life. Salvation and revenge in one. Just like in the books. And that's not all. I was so hurt and angry, I did something else, something I regret terribly to this day. That next day, after you tied the black armband on me, I went out on the street because I felt suffocated inside the house. That's when I saw Dhana. She asked me if you were home. She had a letter for you. I told her you were already asleep and to give me the letter. I told her I'd give it to you in the morning. But I was so disgusted by what you'd done, I never gave you the letter. It stayed in the inner pocket of my vest. And I ran away that night. Back then, I thought you didn't deserve to be happy, and this would be my revenge. I wanted to keep you from the happiness you and Dhana had. I no longer feel this way. Every person deserves to be happy. You included, despite what you did. I forgive you. I'm putting Dhana's letter in this envelope and I beg you for forgiveness.

Something good has come out of all this, after all. I saw Dhana on the bus yesterday. It turns out we live in adjacent neighborhoods. She's even more beautiful than I remembered. We recognized each other and exchanged a couple of words. She asked me how you are. I told her we haven't spoken in many years. This is what prompted me to send you her letter. The meeting left an awful taste in my mouth. I felt like someone who had ruined the lives of two people who could have been happy together. Forgive me, Bekija. The terrible actions of the past are the most dangerous landslide of the present.

Still . . . I took Dhana's number under the pretext that we'd get together for coffee one day. She told me she was leaving in a few days to go to a writer's residency in London. I'm not sure for how long. Maybe she'll even stay there. She said she didn't want to live in Sofia anymore. The city and the people were suffocating her, she said. Bekija, please, come be with me, even if not for me, do it for her. You are always welcome in my home. Think of yourself. No one has to die this time. Just simply come. You have my phone number and my address. I'll wait for you, regardless of whether you choose to come or not.

P.S. If you do decide to come, hurry, she leaves in two weeks and you won't be able to see each other after that.

Sále
January 1, 2018
Sofia, Bulgaria

The Lie

Dhana's words, holes in the bus's filthy curtains, and the familiar pain in my stomach, there ever since I can remember, ever since

I will love you forever
I will love you forever

what you do to yourself—no one else can do to you

you did this to yourself you dumb bitch, sixteen years in the trap of your own contrivances

if there's one thing you can't get back it's time, daddy's boy, there's your son now, Murash

there, isn't this what you wanted, isn't that what I wanted

Hi, Bekija, I saw your father at the river today, he was washing sheepskins with your mother and Sále. The stench traveled the entire bed of the river. Your father told me that you are happy, that you're getting married and that you've been looking forward to it for a long time. That you love your betrothed, that he comes from a good family and all that, that you love him the way only a woman can love a man. Is it true? Last night at the dairy, I came away thinking something else entirely, for a fleeting moment I felt as though you were mine.

the lie is a worm

Is it true, Bekija, do you really love him, why did you lie to me?

the lie is a worm

the next words in Dhana's letter make me wish the bus would sink into the ditch on the side of the road, I want to prostrate myself over the seat like sheepskin and to never again hear any words, only the radio in the ditch, the incessant radio, when you think about it, even if you broke your head the thoughts would never stop pounding inside it, sixteen years, sixteen years, babo Tsane, is Dhana coming back for the summer

I don't know who to believe anymore, you or your father. I don't know anything anymore. I'm lost without you, Bekija. If what Murash said, that you love Nemanja and everything else, is a lie, come to the dairy tonight and run away with me to Bulgaria. You deserve better than this arranged marriage. We'll get a place of our own and we'll live there, just the two of us. I'll read to you every day and we'll drink milk, I promise you. Just come back with me, please, Bekija. Tell me it's all a lie.

what you do to yourself—no one else can do to you

I told her you were already sleeping, give me the letter, I'll give it to her in the morning, Bekija, if you don't come tonight, I'll leave for Bulgaria and

I'll never again return
I'll never again return
I'll never again return
I'll never again return

I'm coming, my love

the bus rocks my body, something sprouts in my stomach, it's not a weed

I know what it is, it's a flower, it has thorns and it's called Dhana

Eternally yours,
Dhana

The White Dove

the revolving door turns and from its wings the passengers emerge, flocking in from the arrivals wing, some carry duffel bags, others backpacks, purses, plastic bags, children, just outside the door, about ten meters from it, stands a young man, dressed in a brown jacket and dark-blue jeans, actually, his clothes have absolutely no relevance, everyone at the bus station is wearing clothes, it's just that he's the only one with a sign that says *Bekija*, the young man is Sále, he's waiting for his sister, they haven't seen each other in so long that the young man wonders whether he'll even recognize her, he holds the sign in one hand, will I recognize her, the other hand is in his jacket pocket, which is also not important because the more important thing right now is that the hand clutching the sign is damp from squeezing it, and if he were to remove his hand from the sign, the young man's fingers would leave wet marks, he's not thinking about the wet marks, he's wondering what he'll say to his sister, how will he recognize her, how will she be dressed, things that would be irrelevant for anyone else but him, he wishes to escape the moment of awkwardness between a brother and a sister who've long ago sentenced each other to death, will he be the one to ask her for forgiveness right there, or will she ask him when they get home, will they begin talking about this right there at the bus station or on the way home, will they even bring up the whole thing, the revolving door turns time by sixteen years and through it comes an effeminate man with short hair slicked to one side, he enters the carousel of the door dressed in an old-fashioned dress, his shoes are white patent leather with short heels, he's clumsy and heavy on his heeled feet, it must be from the shoes, the door's wings nudge him forward, this makes his knees bend, he almost sits on his heels, it must be from the door, people often think it's from the shoes but it's from the door, the door is like life

once you enter the revolving door nobody asks you where you're off to, the wings spin and you must move forward, you must not lag behind, you must not be too quick, if you force the carousel the back wing can push you and trip you, if you can't balance the correct tempo and you get your directions confused you can get really hurt, attention

the young man's eyes meet Sále's eyes, their eyes are the same, their noses too, they are siblings, this can be observed by anyone who doesn't know them who passes by them and would only note, these two people are related, they are brother and sister, nothing more, and they would continue on their way, the young man in the dress carries the name written on the sign, the young man is a woman, despite the fact she looks like a boy, the soft outlines of her face reveal this, the woman exits the carousel, the door's wing pushes her forward and she falls to the floor, her heavy backpack pinning her to the ground, she lies on the floor and doesn't get up as though she has not an ounce of strength to do so, Sále rushes to her, someone looking on would think he's rushing to her to get her up, lift her off the ground, but no, he goes to her, gets down on his knees and hugs her, tightly squeezes her around the waist, he has no intention of lifting her off the ground, the floor is frigid, as it is every day, but on this day it doesn't matter, because a brother and a sister are embracing each other tightly and they're sobbing with pain and joy, not saying anything, whatever words might be said right now won't have any meaning against the backdrop of this painting that tears up a stout woman nearby whose backside is dressing the small betting stool she's squeezed herself onto, Eurochance, you win, madam, but if you had doubled your bet, you would now be two hundred leva richer, not just twenty, the woman is sniffling and melting with tenderness, if you'd bet double, she doesn't answer the croupier, the brother and the sister are still in an embrace on the ground and they aren't moving, the stout woman turns and bets everything on the highest odds, brave, very brave, madam, today she saw God and understood there is nothing left to lose, from today onward nothing will be the same, the door turns and through it emerges the next wave of arrivals and with them a white dove enters, crashes into the head of one of the passengers but manages to escape out of the door, touches down on the station's clock, the stout woman sees it and wipes her nose with her sleeve, the next round of betting is coming up

The Right Side of the Armoire

the towels are in the bathroom, there's shampoo and soap in the cabinet above the sink, you can find clean clothes in the left side of the armoire, they belong to a friend, she comes over all the time and left some of her things here, plus you're the same height, her clothes should fit you

the first blast from the shower is cold, I think this ought to wake me from the dream I've chosen to dream, the water slowly gets hotter, reddens my skin and each thought births the next, they step on each other, trip, leap and catch up to each other, jump and overtake one another, they flash like the billboards around town, so many lights, how do these people live like this, and this incessant noise, thousands of cars, filled with thoughts, flying along the crevices of my brain

you can get used to anything, even yourself

hi, Bekija, I saw your father today at the river, he was washing sheepskins with your mother and Sále, I don't know who to believe anymore, you or your father, I don't know anything anymore, I'm lost without you, is it true, Bekija, do you love him, why did you lie to me, I will love you forever, the steam in the bathroom is thick as fog, it makes it impossible to see myself in the mirror, I wipe it with my hand, I saw Dhana on the bus yesterday, it turns out we're neighbors, she's even more beautiful than before, stop it, girl, this kind of thinking will kill you, I've always thought more than I needed to, are other people like me or am I one of the ones not right in the head, I twist the faucet and the thoughts stop

there are women's clothes in the left side of the armoire, they're my brother's friend's clothes, she comes over a lot, apparently, we are the same height, he said, no, I open the right side of the armoire instead, it's where Sále's clothes are diligently folded, I smell them, I do what I do and I close the door, I open the door to the kitchen, my brother stares at me, frozen, he's sitting at the table with two cups of tea, I am wearing his clothes, a pair of trousers with a belt and a button-down shirt, my brother bursts out laughing, then he feels bad about it and stops laughing, he's only smiling now, I knew it, I knew you'd get dressed in these, how did you know, I just knew, there are things you know and you don't need to guess, like the fact that now you're called Matija, I am Matija now, yes, you told me many times when we were little that if you had been born a boy, you'd want to be called

Matija, yes, I assumed that you'd chosen that name when you became a sworn virgin, I'm so happy you came, here, I made you tea

I think about how it's always easier to offer someone tea rather than to discuss the things that truly matter, tea is easier than challenging life and coming to terms with the fact that you're not as strong as you make yourself out to be

do you want to talk, why, I think everything that needed to be said has already been said in those letters, and if I'm here, this means, this means that you're staying here, right, I don't know, I don't know what to do with my life, this is what scares me, I don't know what to do with myself, I don't want to go back there, I know that much, have you ever seen someone try to outrun their shadow, I haven't, that's why I accept the fact it drags itself behind me like a heavy chain, there's room for you here and your chain, you can stay as long as you like, I live by myself, you won't be in the way, I can help you find a job and

Sále continues with the usual things, work, the apartment, the market, the public transportation, the store, the sales and the discounts, you'll feel so much better here than if you'd stayed back there, when will he finally get to the real point

look, I know you're not really here because of me, says Sále and my stomach begins to hurt, I know you came because of her, I get up and go to the sink, I turn on the cold water all the way and begin to drink, I feel the water enter my body, I feel it sever my body in half, my stomach continues to hurt, the pain gets louder, an unfamiliar pain, a powerful pain, are you okay, did this have to happen right now, Bekija, are you alright, I can only nod, my movements are constricted, some kind of flower with thorns is stuck in my throat and I'm waiting on my brother to call it by its name, he will surely say it, Bekija, just tell me when and I'll call

Dhana

Dhana passes through my body like a razor, doubles me over, drags me to the ground, when the pain is as strong as this, your senses refuse their normal function, you start seeing black, the back of your neck tightens, your breathing quickens and you lose track of time, finally, right before you pass out, you feel as though the pain almost vanishes, you suddenly drift off and hear only torn fragments of speech, like

this is an emergency, quick, please send an ambulance
or, Dhana, I'm sorry to bother you, this is Sále

Fetus in Fetu

Bekija

the light from the windows cuts into the backs of the eyes, the room is blinding white, it smells like the medicine drawer in our house, a blurry silhouette murmurs my name, I know this voice, where am I, this voice was exactly what I needed, is that you, Dhana, I want to say but I'm unable to open my mouth, I raise my finger and she infers from it what she requires, yes, it's me, Dhana, the silhouette sharpens and leaning over me is the most beautiful woman in the world, am I hallucinating, she suddenly wraps her arms around me and my face sinks into her hair, her hair smells like the hair of a woman who washes it every day, her face is soft, her cheek is wet and presses against mine, I don't move, she pulls back sharply, as though someone's told her to and she sits on the chair by my bed, Sále called me, he said you were complaining of sharp pains in your stomach, I came as soon as I could, I didn't think after all these years we'd be seeing each other in a hospital

don't leave

humans and their bottomless needs, what abject beings we are, people, we're not so good at dying alone, it's fear that's to blame for it all, love plays us for fools, whenever she feels like it, she calls us on the phone, asks uncomfortable questions, she begs, I feel strange, I can no longer feel the flower and its thorns in my stomach, I feel nothing but Dhana's shampoo on my face, what happened

you're recovering from a very complex surgery, a medical miracle, I'm serious, here, look, Dhana takes out a newspaper

I don't ask her what happened to me, I speak about the two of us, this means going over what happened to us, but she doesn't understand me, the years are a precipice, Dhana acts like an acquaintance, what else should I expect, but no, no, I can see it, her hands are shaking and the newspaper trembles in her long fingers, her eyes are wet, I've got something in my eye, she says, she must have a reason to lie, I know it is me, I am the thing in your eye, the thing that has been scratching for sixteen years, I think, Dhana reads

TERRIFYING DISCOVERY: TWIN LIVES INSIDE HIS SISTER FOR 33 YEARS

A 33-year-old woman was admitted to St. Sofia Hospital due to severe abdominal pain. The surgeons expected to find an oversized tumor, but instead discovered the remnants of a partially formed twin, inside the woman since birth. This is an extremely rare medical phenomenon.

The condition, known as fetus in fetu, occurs inside the womb when one fetus becomes trapped inside the other and forms a connection to it. The mass, found inside the woman's abdominal cavity, weighed 1.8 kg and had bones, hair, and teeth, as well as a growth resembling an umbilical cord. The 'host twin,' in this case, the woman, is considered the stronger twin, while the other is deemed the weaker one. In simple terms, the dominant twin, the woman, "consumed" her brother in their mother's womb. The fetus was successfully removed, and the woman is recovering.

I want to get out of here, I can't take another death that is my fault, it's not my fault, right, Dhana, this isn't my fault too, tell me, am I guilty of this too, am I a murderer, still in my mother's womb I heard things like I want a boy, now everything's crystal clear, my mother pregnant with twins, a boy and a girl, that was the boy, the whole village is talking, she's not carrying like it's a boy, she's not carrying like it's a girl either, it's neither here nor there, my mother bleeds in the bathroom, my father's mother's incantations, this girl can't be born, let it be just the boy who is born, to continue the family name, you don't want a girl, Murash

Dhana holds me again, she's naive, she believes her embrace will stop my tears and bring back my dead twin brother, I deserve all of it, from the first death to the last death, fratricide is a sin, I don't deserve to live, murderers don't deserve to live, I'm leaving, Dhana stops me by grabbing my arms and holding me to her, her hands are warm, like bread, this whole time my father had another son, only that son was inside of me, I carried him inside of me for thirty-three years, the son was inside of me this whole time, I was the real son, wasn't I

all desperately desired things materialize
one way or another

still in my mother's womb I heard things like my father saying, please, doctor, do something, I'm sorry, sir, the boy isn't here, but luckily, the female fetus is in very good health, better than good even, and if it continues to develop like this, you will have a healthy and strong baby girl, daddy's boy, stay with me, Dhana raises her hands and they're filled by my face, I cry for a long time, then she cries with me, and then we sit in silence, she lies down next to me on the bed and holds me

you are not to blame for any of this, she says
you are not to blame for the fact you were born a woman
there's one thing a person can't be guilty of and that is of having been born

then we sleep

Molehills

Dhana came to see me every day during visiting hours and brought me good food, the hospital gave us only yogurt and two slices of bread, not to mention that I had to be on a special diet because of my stomach, and, of course, Dhana came with a book every day, we had two hours together, we didn't discuss anything else, she sat on the chair next to my bed and read to me, there were so many things I wanted to say to her but I preferred to listen to her read, to listen to her voice and die, the rest of the time I felt like I was losing my mind lying here in this room, yes, if I were to remain in this room there's no doubt in my mind I'd go crazy, the doctors won't let me go, in room six there's a terribly anxious woman, she wants to leave too, what are we supposed to do, doctor, she wants to leave, if she wants to leave so bad, she should pay her way, please, Dhana, tell them to let me go, give this woman a sedative already, we gave her some already, then why is she still raging, up the dosage, Dhana, please

don't go

the more you want something to be over so you can leave, the more time clings to you and refuses to let go, is that the woman from room six again, she's grown immune to the sedatives, that poor nurse, it must not be easy for her anyway, and on top of everything she has to deal with my hysterics too, only when Dhana read to me was I able to forget about the days when the old lady snored next to me, the rest of the time she would not stop talking, do you have kids, are you married, does your husband respect you, my silence is not enough to shut her up, here people have no manners, they don't care that you want to get some sleep, should I turn down the television, it's probably bothering you, nothing bothers me, only I bother me, I bother only myself, where's Dhana, get Dhana here, I don't care what time it is, call her

I'm here, Bekija

two more days and you'll be able to go home, uttering the words is always the easiest thing, people go back to their homes, I don't have a home, home is where, don't talk like that, Sále is expecting you at his place, and your husband must be worried about you and expecting you to get home, you have not said anything about him since you've been here

there are conversations that can't be avoided with the reading of books or the drinking of tea

Dhana gets up and goes to the window, she watches the pigeon on the windowsill, her eyes fill with seawater, she doesn't turn around because she knows if she turns around she'll fill up the room with the same water and we'll both drown, I have no husband, I say, and the pigeon flies off, didn't you get married, no, why do you think I look more like a boy than a girl, I have no idea, I don't know anything about you since, turn around, look at me

do I look like a woman who has a man, I am a man, Dhana, my body is just a detail, Dhana doesn't turn around, I became a sworn virgin after you left, your letter reached me, do you know when, do you know *when* your letter reached me, two days ago, that horror, here it is, visible to the naked eye, it scales your body, starts at the heels and crawls upward, it grabs you by the throat, your eyes grow large, the body coils in the opposite direction, in the wrong direction, in the direction of the past, if you want to ruin your life right this second, go back into the awful past, how can you have received it two days ago, you don't know anything, that night, the same night you and I, everything changed that night and I didn't marry Nemanja, do you really think I could have done it, I love you, Dhana, Dhana slowly grows younger in front of my eyes, her hair shortens, her face rosies up, the time machine is set in motion and we are both seventeen again, the room darkens, I can smell the flour, our scars glow in the dark, we can finally see each other again

the eye of the water snake is a hook, my love
the eye of the water snake is an ear

after that night at the dairy everything went to hell, you don't know the laws of the Kanun, you're not obligated to know them, but you and I did something that pulled the rope on my entire family, this doesn't mean I regret what happened, that night was the most beautiful night of my life but at the same time it was the most awful night of my life, because the Kanun decrees that if the bride isn't a virgin on her wedding night her husband must kill her, Dhana sobs and buries her face in her palms, she finally understands, I know the emotions that must be going through her, the feeling is akin to wading through tall grass and knowing that if there's no one nearby to pull you out, you will sink, why didn't you stop me, Bekija, if you knew what was coming, how could I stop the most beautiful thing that has ever happened to me, it's not fair, Bekija, you are essentially telling me I was an accomplice to your murder, I want to cease existing, I'm leaving, no, don't leave, you're not to blame for anything, I want you to hear me out, after the dairy I went home and the following night informed my father that I wished to become a sworn virgin, this put into motion a blood feud with Nemanja's family and sentenced a man from my family to death, I had to put the black band on my father's arm or my brother's, I chose my brother, and that night, the same night you came to give me the letter, he chose my death by taking the letter and keeping it from me, he wanted to send me to burn in hell where I belong, he ran away in the middle of the night, Dhana can't hold back her tears, she sobs, the old hag in the room hacks and her snoring goes down a decibel, and after Sále ran away, my father tied the black armband on himself and they killed him, I don't want to listen to this anymore, a month ago a journalist came to the house, she wanted to interview me because I was apparently the last remaining sworn virgin in these lands, that's when I took out the letters I'd been getting from Sále all these years, but you know, you know that I can't read, my darling, the last letter contained your letter, Dhana throws herself on me and cries, she cries the way people cry when they realize that as much as they might want to, they can't turn back time, nothing has changed for me, Dhana, nothing has changed for me either, Bekija, there's not a day that, the words come out on their own, without being called, all these years, stacked inside of us like molehills

I love you
I love you

there's not a day goes by that

Dhana's hand clenches my mouth, Dhana's hand is now an inextricable part of my face, I take this hand and this body as my own, we cry and kiss each other's faces, we crisscross our enfloured hands, our hair pleats into one braid, the blanket of night covers us, hides us from the entire world

tonight below that same blanket two souls with tears in their eyes will knead the softest bread

The Zipper of the Sky

the light piercing the window blinds cuts through my eyes, I'm alone in the bed, there's a piece of paper on the nightstand, should I die now or later, I'm forbidden from getting up, I get up, I take the piece of paper and make my way over to the old hag in the bed next to me, I shake her bed to wake her up, which she does, what is the matter with you, girl, have you lost your mind or what, read this, leave me alone, girl, read it to me now, I must resemble a serial killer of old grandmas, I don't care, you young people have no respect for your elders, read, she reaches for her glasses, I hand them to her, I don't understand anything, this letter isn't in Bulgarian, I don't understand you either, leave me alone, the old woman yells and throws the letter on the floor, I bend down to pick it up, the door opens, they've probably heard all the yelling, it's Sále, Bekija, what's the matter, I say nothing, I get up and push the letter into his hands, read this

Good morning, Bekija,

I mentioned that I'm leaving for a writer's residency, but what I didn't mention is that yesterday was my last day here and today I fly to England. My contract with the residency is for at least a year, with the option of extending my stay. Please forgive my choosing to part like this and for not saying goodbye to you properly but I simply assumed that the best thing for both of us would be to avoid this mutually excruciating moment. The dawn did not dissipate my feelings of guilt for all the terrible things that befell you and your family. I don't believe that I deserve this love and I don't deserve to know happiness. It must be written for you and me to be eternally separated by something, and to shoulder the responsibility before God for every indirect murder we've committed. We're bound to bear the consequences. The last few days were some of the most beautiful of my life. You took me back to my childhood and to that fairy-tale naivete where love exists outside of guilt and all else.

That was us, and the ritual of reconciliation between our souls could not be described more beautifully—late at night and early in the morning, when the hands leave their clocks, and time is nothing but a detail, a blemish on the visage of a planet that, anytime I gaze into your eyes, you make me question whether is even turning.

Last night you were mine again, you gave yourself to me as if for the first time and that was all that mattered, in this bed, both of us wrapped in cotton seaweed, nearly awake in the eruption of the volcano in the pillow, and nearly asleep in the pleasure of the touch of two bodies becoming one, this one single body touches only itself, and it finds that it is enough.

If I were with you now, and we raised the window blinds, we would see how the crane over Sofia unzips the sky and the light enters the room like a blissful cat, like a sun lion we refuse to battle, as we cover each other with our hands.

We're not ready, we've never been ready to accept life outside this room as our separation, to rise from the bed and dissolve into the everyday like characters from a Duras novel, who search for each other their whole lives and, in the evening of their days, find each other—by phone or in the loud headline of a newspaper.

I don't know how to rise from the waves of your twisted body, pointing toward the shore; your moan is like a bird foretelling an island—we are saved, or almost, I don't want, I don't want this shore, the shore in the gaze of cross-eyed ladies at the counters where we pay our bills, water meters with numbers in their eyes, a rain of labels pouring down on us, an earring, the earring of the day is made of tin, brined cheese, a new price—you forgot your change, ma'am.

I am far away from you now. Hundreds of kilometers most likely, but I am still in your boat. Your hair rocks me like a drowning man, glimpsed by chance by a fisherman when the fish has, unexpectedly, stopped pulling, the salt in my hair comes from your tears, so I won't be lost to you again, so I won't sink into our shared oblivion, for a moment, nothing else matters—passion's joined vessels spill their cement, and you and I, my love, remain walled into this bed, the only refuge of our childhood, its knees scraped but still joyful, its ball flies off and is stopped by a monument—this is the monument of our love, of two souls fused into one, destined always to roam the world alone, as two halves.

This is us, and the ritual of our souls' reconciliation could not be described more beautifully—two clock hands shoot out of their timepiece and pierce the celestial hemisphere.

I will miss you, as I always have.

Eternally yours,
Dhana

The Return

the road twists like a water snake, the bus rocks my body as though some body in it has died, I hear an unfamiliar song on the radio, man is a sorry being, he thinks he can outrun his life, once caught in its jaws there's no running, I am one of those people born without a gender and without a place, I was just lucky to remain alive, my name means she who lived, she who remained alive, she who saved herself, nonsense, it's all made up, I am my father's biggest lie, the semitrucks on the road measure out the circles of my hell, if the bus were to veer into the ditch on the side of the road, I could take a breather from myself, from my thoughts, which are relentless, a bird crashes into the bus window, the bus is stopped by a conductor, he climbs onboard to check if anybody's traveling without a ticket, I hand him mine, it's been punched way too many times, but he lets me ride on anyway, so I continue on, toward the place where I'm headed, toward the place where I supposedly belong, home is where your wings got clipped

Bekija, are you sure you don't want to stay with me, no, Sále, I'm leaving, there's no place for me here, people like me have no place anywhere, don't talk like that, you know you can always count on me, I can take a leave of absence from work soon and come visit you, you can count on it

goodbye for now

stupid woman, you thought all of a sudden you could be happy someplace else, without wings, this bus is suffocating, you can't breathe, the air here has already been breathed, I'm vacuumed by my own fate, maybe Dhana is right, maybe we both have to take responsibility for our actions, and so what if God put a birthmark on each of us, right where our clavicles met, above the heart, why is loving someone sometimes not enough, where am I supposed to go, who am I supposed to give all this love to, the stray dogs

the bus stops at the corroded bus stop, my stop, I try to get off the bus but just like in a dream, my body resists, the same way it does when you try to run from something, it doesn't want to move forward together with me, it lags, turn the bus around, I want to scream, but what am I supposed to answer when they ask, where to, ma'am, *to nowhere*, where I belong, I get off, the door closes behind me, the Albanian air ruffles my hair, I must resemble a donkey in this dress and these shoes, I take off the patent leather shoes and throw them in the field, they fly off like birds in the sky, then fall, one after the other

separately

now I know how birds die, all alone

I continue on barefoot
this is how you go to see God
I'm coming, daddy

God

I don't understand
can you help me understand
what this means
hold on, let me listen to the news
and then this:
breaking news
a girl hanged herself
with her umbilical cord

now I know where the madness of lust can bring us, the fear of death, anger, envy, jealousy, and every other feeling that holds no peace, comes from the shadows, forces you to make bad decisions, to eat yourself alive, to eat others alive, to eat your own brother alive, I unlock the front door, everything inside is exactly how I left it, except for me, in the middle of the room there are the letters and the photographs, a pile of ashes, how could I have done that, look what you did, how could you, my life is a pile of ashes, I want to die

my trousers, where are my trousers and my shoes, where are they, I quickly pull the legs of the trousers and my working boots, I'm doing something with my hands so that I don't lose it, I put on the trousers and the boots, a freak, look at yourself

below the waist, a man
above the waist, a woman

just look at yourself, the shouting an attempt to silence the thoughts and my collapse to the floor, the floor is cold, I have no tears left for this floor, my will to live has desiccated completely, I scream and then fall silent, I have nothing left to call for

quiet now

you hear that, my thoughts thin out and silence is coming, it's beginning to get real quiet, very quiet and very warm, do you see the big silence, do you hear the boundless quietude, when you've lost everything, *God, is that you*, tell me your name, do you hear the cow's bellowing, the crickets in the grass, the goats' bells in the pastures, a walnut falls somewhere in the dead leaves, a pigeon flies away, tranquility possesses me, I am a small leafy branch being carried away by the river, *is that you,* I know that it's you, wait for me, I'm coming with you into the light, I take the small stool and the rope from the wall, I'm coming, daddy

a woman gets off the bus, she's carrying only a small bit of luggage, she takes off that way, the way the heart leads, she's going off memory, the heart remembers the wolf trails of the soul, she passes the water mill, she can hear the laughter of children, then she walks past the dairy and hears whispering inside, then along the river where someone's washing sheepskins in the current, she's heading toward someone

she stops in front of the door marked by a small cross carved into it, she doesn't knock, she enters without so much as calling out, she's looking for someone who no longer belongs to this house, Bekija, are you here, the house is silent, the only thing making a sound is the cow, the woman heads toward it, the direction of the bellowing, the door to the cow's stable is open, she puts her hand on her mouth as soon as she crosses the threshold, she sobs, wildly, because of what her eyes see, it is the last thing she thought she would see crossing this threshold

Bekija sits on the little stool, in her hands she holds a rope, the other end of the rope binds the front legs of a newborn calf, steam rises from its small wet body, the cow licks the calf and her tongue topples it over every time it attempts to stand

Bekija, the woman who's come off the bus cries out, the woman who's headed to where my name means she who lives, she who remains alive, she who has saved herself, Bekija looks to the woman, then to the newborn calf, she cries, she smiles and she cries, the two cry and laugh together, Bekija gets up and goes to embrace the woman, the two stay holding each other for a long time, they say nothing, the calf finds its mother's teat and begins to suckle noisily, a fly lands on its left ear, the cow keeps licking her child and it is precisely there, by this picture and in this moment that the two women feel immortality, they've discovered joy and in this joy there is love, and in the center of this love is the immeasurable, that, which is eternal, that, which cannot be called by name

Bulgarian poet, writer, screenwriter, actor, and playwright RENE KARABASH (b. Irena Ivanova) has won multiple awards for her work, including several Best Actress awards for her role in the film Godless and the Elias Canetti prize—Bulgaria's most prestigious literary award—for *She Who Remains*, her debut novel. *She Who Remains* has been translated into over a dozen languages, including French, Italian, Swedish, Portuguese, and Arabic, and a film based on Karabash's adaptation of the novel is being produced. Karabash is also the author of *Omar's Letters to His Future Wife*.

IZIDORA ANGEL is a Bulgarian-born memoirist and literary translator based in Chicago, Illinois. Her translations from Bulgarian include Hristo Karastoyanov's *The Same Night Awaits Us All*, Nataliya Deleva's *Four Minutes*, and Yordanka Beleva's *Keder*, for which she received a National Endowment for the Arts Fellowship. Angel's work has appeared in *A Public Space*, *Astra*, *Best Literary Translations 2024*, *Chicago Reader*, *Electric Literature*, *Words Without Borders*, and elsewhere. She received a PEN/Heim Translation Fund Grant and the Gulf Coast Prize in Translation for her in-progress work on *She Who Remains*. Angel is at work on a memoir, first excerpted in *The American Scholar*.

About Sandorf Passage

Sandorf Passage publishes work that creates a prismatic perspective on what it means to live in a globalized world. It is a home to writing inspired by both conflict zones and the dangers of complacency. All Sandorf Passage titles share in common how the biggest and most important ideas are best explored in the most personal and intimate of spaces.